LADY ROSEANNE

LADY ROSEANNE

JENNY OLDFIELD

Illustrated by
Paul Hunt

Hodder
Children's
Books

a division of Hodder Headline Limited

With thanks to Bob, Karen and Katie Foster, and to the staff and
guests at Lost Valley Ranch, Deckers, Colorado

Copyright © 2001 Jenny Oldfield
Illustrations copyright © 2001 Paul Hunt

First published in Great Britain in 2001
by Hodder Children's Books

The right of Jenny Oldfield to be identified as the author of
this work has been asserted by her in accordance with the
Copyright, Designs and Patents Act 1988.

10 9 8 7 6 5 4 3 2 1

A Catalogue record for this book is available from the British Library

ISBN 0 340 79171 3

Typeset by Avon Dataset Ltd, Bidford-on-Avon, Warks

Printed and bound in Great Britain by
The Guernsey Press Co. Ltd, Channel Isles

Hodder Children's Books
a division of Hodder Headline Limited
338 Euston Road
London NW1 3BH

1

'Hey, Cornbread, quit it!' Kirstie Scott shook her boot to make the creamy-yellow kitten let go of the lace.

The playful little cat hung on as if his life depended on it. Suspended in mid air, he grabbed Kirstie's ankle with his front paws and went on worrying at the snaking lace.

'Yeah, yeah, very cute!' she sighed. 'You're a big, brave kitty and I'm impressed. But Mom's orders are for me to sweep out this tack-room real good. She wants the whole place spotless

1

before the new wrangler gets here later tonight.'

Cornbread ignored her and went on wrestling her bootlace. A recent arrival at Half-Moon Ranch, he'd turned up out of the blue and attached himself to Kirstie. Soon he'd become as much a part of the set-up as the thirty or so horses out in Red Fox Meadow.

Adorable – yeah. Especially with those big blue-grey eyes. The only problem was, the kitten didn't like to work.

'Cornbread, I don't have time to play right now!' Kirstie insisted. She leaned the big yard brush against the wall then stooped to detach him from her ankle. Holding him high in the air, she shook him gently. 'I've got work to do, OK?'

As she lowered him to the dusty floor, picked up her broom and went on sweeping, Kirstie thought ahead to the arrival of the new wrangler.

These last couple of months had been difficult for her mom, who – as a female head of a dude ranch in the foothills of the Rocky Mountains – had her work cut out at the best of times. For a start, Charlie Miller had upped and left to go back to college and leave his wrangling days behind. His replacement, Troy Hendren with his brilliant cutting and reining horse, Silver Spur, had been a gas. But he hadn't lasted long before he'd been headhunted by the boss of a working cattle ranch out in Montana.

Then Hadley had had his accident. The old timer had risked his life to save his blue roan horse and landed in hospital with a busted leg and collar bone.

Kirstie paused amidst a cloud of dust while Cornbread pounced on her broom. She glanced through the door to see the old wrangler limping slowly across the corral. 'Hey, Hadley!' she called.

'Hey,' he replied in his usual low growl. 'Did the new guy show up yet?'

'Nope. Not until suppertime was what I heard.' She grinned as the kitten left off attacking the broom and turned to chase a stray leaf that had blown in through the open door.

'You know anythin' about him?' Hadley asked. Since his accident, he'd moved stiffly and slowly, grumbling about the length of time it took for his old bones to heal. He said it was all he could do to get out to the meadow to spend time with Moondance, the horse for whom he'd almost lost his life.

'Nope,' Kirstie said again.

'So what's the big mystery?' the old man quizzed. 'How come Sandy ain't sayin' nothin?'

'Dunno.' Kirstie went on with her job, brushing out the dark corners of the tack-room and under the long rows of saddles and bridles. 'All I know is, Mom drove over to Denver to meet him off the plane.'

'Where did she find him? Did she advertise the position? Has the guy had experience working on a dude ranch?' Reluctant to drop the subject, Hadley gave Kirstie the third degree.

'Hey, what's the big deal?' Trying to assure the ex-wrangler that her mom knew what she was doing after five years of running the ranch single-handed, Kirstie threatened to sweep Cornbread up with the dirt. 'Go on, scat!' she told the mischievous kitten.

'Huh!' Hadley frowned, evidently unhappy that Sandy hadn't conferred with him over the hiring of a new hand. He turned and limped off, heading out to the ramuda to find his beloved Moondance.

It wasn't long afterwards that Kirstie heard the sound of horses returning to the corral. Glancing out of the window, she spied her brother, Matt, and his new girlfriend, Lauren Booth. Matt was riding Cadillac, his big cream-coloured thoroughbred, and Lauren was on her beautiful little Appaloosa, Lady Roseanne.

Yeah, love's young dream! Kirstie said to herself. There was no denying the romance of the picture the young couple presented. Matt sat tall, dark and handsome in his saddle, his black stetson pulled well down against the October wind. But in terms of glamour, Lauren easily outstripped him, with her long, jet black hair and tight-fitting beige leather jacket and blue jeans. The jacket was fringed along the seams, giving Lauren a cool Native American look. So did the horse, come to think of it.

The Appie was something else. Like a horse from the old western movies: supple, swift and beautifully marked. Her white coat was covered in chocolate-brown spots, scattered mostly over her back and legs. And like all Appaloosas she had a touch of the wild plains horse – the long legs, the flared nostrils, the streaming white mane and tail.

Kirstie could easily picture Lady Roseanne

standing on a ridge in the sunset. The camera would close in on her and her buckskin-clad rider. They would look noble yet savage, wild as the wind . . .

Get real! she told herself. Catching her own reflection in the tack-room window, she saw a dirty, dust-covered figure in an old baseball cap and denim shirt. So she decided to stay where she was and let Lauren and Matt say their goodbyes in peace.

Hearing the clink of Matt's spurs as he dismounted, Kirstie tried in vain to block her ears to the smoochy talk that was bound to follow.

'You OK?' Matt asked as he helped Lauren down from her saddle.

'Sure.' The break in Lauren's voice told Kirstie that this wasn't true. 'I guess I feel kinda sad, that's all.'

' 'Cos it's our last ride out together before you have to leave?' Matt's sensitive side came out for a change. He seemed to pick up what his girlfriend meant and be feeling the same way.

'Yeah. The mountains are so pretty in the Fall,' Lauren murmured. Her voice came over muffled now, as if she'd leaned her head against Matt's shoulder.

'Oh, so Eagle's Peak is the only thing you're gonna miss during your trip to Europe?'

Cheesy! Kirstie thought, as Matt fished for more.

'No way!' Lauren decided to tease him. 'I'm gonna miss Big Macs and Pizza Huts . . .'

'They have them in Europe!' Matt protested.

'OK, I'll miss the aspen trees turning red and losing their leaves. I'll pine to know how the Giants are progressing in the basketball league. Oh, and most of all I'll miss Lady Roseanne!'

Way to go, Lauren! Kirstie's opinion was that her brother was already too big for his boots.

'What about me?' Forced to ask the straight question, Matt sounded like a young kid. 'Are you gonna e-mail me while you're gone?'

'Maybe . . .' After a short pause, Lauren added, 'Yeah, naturally I'll keep in touch. If I leave Roseanne here at Half-Moon Ranch, I'll need to check in to see how she's doing!'

Hmm. That was the first Kirstie had heard about them child-minding Lauren's Appie while she went travelling. *Good thinking, Matt.* She had to hand it to her brother for finding a clever way to hold on to his new and very beautiful girlfriend.

'Yeah, but will you miss me?' Matt demanded.

Through the small window Kirstie could see that Lauren's final answer had come in the shape of a big hug followed by a lingering kiss. *Jeez!* she thought. *Let me out of here!* But it was too late; she was trapped and forced to witness the gooey stuff.

'It'll only be until Christmas,' Lauren promised. 'Then I'll be back.'

More kisses. More blushes from the tack-room. Kirstie wondered whether to clatter her broom against the doorpost to alert them to the fact that they had a witness.

'And you promise you'll take good care of Lady Roseanne?' Lauren extricated herself from Matt's arms. She turned to fuss over the gentle-natured Appie, letting the mare nip mint candy from the palm of her hand.

'She'll get the full, four-diamond treatment,' Matt promised. 'I'll treat her like she was my own horse – give her the pick of the alfalfa, brush and curry her every day . . .

Fat chance! Kirstie thought. In her own mind she knew that Matt would hand over these everyday chores to his everloving sister.

'. . . ride her out, work her to keep her from getting fat. Hey, and don't forget I'm training to be a vet. So I'll pick up the least little problem before it has chance to develop. Satisfied?'

Lauren nodded and put her arms round his neck. 'I will miss you so much, Matt Scott!' she whispered.

'And I'll miss you too, Lauren Booth.'

At that precise moment, a flurry of yellow leaves swept in through the tack-room door, carried by the blustery wind. Cornbread thought he was in cat heaven as they whirled and spun over his head. He jumped and twisted, rolled and sprinted out on to the porch.

The leaves swirled back into the corral. Cornbread chased. They swept towards Cadillac and Lady Roseanne, standing quietly as their riders said their fond farewells. Risking life and limb, the kitten chased the dry leaves between the horses' legs.

Wham! Cadillac lifted a hindleg and brought his solid hoof crashing down. Cornbread escaped with inches to spare, then shot off towards the barn.

Lauren gasped, then sighed with relief.

'That's one of his nine lives used up!' Matt joked.

High time to quit the lovey-dovey stuff, unsaddle the horses then drive the lovely Lauren back into town.

'So where's Mom?' Matt asked as he sat down to supper. The final parting in San Luis had made him quieter than normal. He seemed thoughtful and a little bit down.

'She phoned from Denver to say she was held up,' Kirstie answered as she served chicken and fries to Matt, Hadley and their head wrangler, Ben Marsh. 'But she should be back real soon.'

Listening to the guys talk about the week ahead, she realised that they were heading into a busy time of year.

'There are twenty-three spring cattle out there in the hills,' Ben reminded Hadley and Matt. 'We need to bring them all in for branding, then push 'em out again for the last month of grazing before the snow comes.'

'Yeah, and early next week, say Monday, we trailer half the ramuda up to Aspen Park for winter pasture,' Matt added.

'Not forgettin' the fences to be fixed, trails to be cleared and a hundred other things around the ranch buildings.' Hadley didn't help to lift the mood. 'That's on top of the new bunch of dudes we get in on Sunday.'

'Maybe I should take a week out of school, stay home and help!' Kirstie suggested brightly.

Matt gave her a you-must-be-joking stare. 'Nice try, Kirstie. I guess the new guy should ease things,' he said to Ben. 'An extra pair of hands is what we need right now.'

Hadley grunted. 'You gotta teach him the ropes first,' he pointed out.

'Yeah well, let's hope the boss made a good choice and the guy learns fast.' Determined to lighten up, Ben attacked his food with a hearty appetite.

'Here comes Mom's car now.' Kirstie recognised the familiar sound of the engine and went out on to the house porch to greet the new arrival. 'Are you coming?' she called to the others.

Forks chinked against plates as the serious business of eating went ahead.

'Suit yourselves,' Kirstie shrugged. She for one

11

was eager to meet their new wrangler.

She waited for her mom to park in the yard before she stepped out from the porch.

The trunk of the car was already open and a figure was leaning in to haul out a big travel bag. Meanwhile, Sandy got out and spied Kirstie.

'Hi, honey!' She gave a bright wave. 'What's for supper? We're starving!'

'Chicken.' Quickly she ran to help. Then she stopped dead in her tracks. She stared from the new wrangler to her mom.

Sandy grinned. 'Let's go inside and make the formal introductions. Are all the guys there?'

Kirstie nodded, then swallowed hard. Wow, were they in for a surprise! She stood to one side to allow the new employee and her mom to get by.

'Go straight in.' Sandy also did the polite thing by hanging back to let the stranger enter first.

Out on the porch, Kirstie heard three forks clatter on to plates. There was a scraping of chairs as the gang stood up to be introduced.

'Hey, guys,' Sandy said, obviously enjoying the stunned silence. She turned to Kirstie and beckoned her inside. 'Kirstie honey, how about you put on the coffee while I introduce Karina to the other members of our team?'

2

Saturday dawned clear and cold. Overnight the temperature had dropped way below zero, bringing a thick coating of white crystals to the grass and trees. Kirstie's boots crunched through the frost as she stepped out across the yard and into the corral.

In spite of the sudden freeze, she was looking forward to what the day would bring. Or rather, she was eager to find out how the guys would handle Karina Cooper.

Kirstie smiled as she thought back to the night before.

'Karina, I'd like you to meet Ben Marsh, our head wrangler, my son Matt and Hadley Crane. Hadley's been here at Half-Moon Ranch since way back when my folks had the place.' Sandy had made the introductions to three stunned men.

'Yeah, sure, I recall you used to talk a lot about Hadley,' Karina had made the connection as she stepped forward to shake hands with each in turn. Her handshake had been firm and brief, her grey-eyed gaze direct. 'Sandy and me go back to school days in San Luis,' she'd explained. 'You might say we grew up together.'

'Before we went our separate ways,' Kirstie's mom had added. Sandy had evidently enjoyed the stunned look on the guys' faces. 'After school I did the boring thing of going to college, taking an office job, getting married. While Karina here went out and became a cowgirl.'

'Pleased to meet you, Karina.' Ben had been the first to get over his surprise that his new wrangler was not some big, burly guy.

Quite the opposite: Karina was small, slim and wiry. Her hair, once obviously dark, was now streaked iron-grey and cut close to her head. She

15

wore big silver hoops in her ears, a piece of chunky silver and turquoise jewellery around her neck and tight-fitting jeans above snakeskin boots.

How come? The unspoken question had hung heavy in the air as Sandy had made a place for Karina at the supper table. Kirstie had appreciated the guys' doubts, since Karina didn't look at first glance like the type to haul heavy logs off trails, hammer fence posts into rocky ground or take on the daily chore of scooping poop from the corral.

But men never took in the finer details. Like the fact that Karina's hands were square and strong, and her tanned skin had the weather-worn look of someone who'd spent their life working outdoors.

Matt's quick exit from the table and Hadley's moody frown had said more clearly than any words that they both thought Sandy had made a big mistake.

Only kind-hearted, polite Ben had stuck around and made the effort to make Karina feel at home. He'd asked her about her last position on a ranch in New Mexico, discovered that her main love was bronc riding and that she held state titles in roping, flanking and tying.

'That's on the women's circuit,' she'd reminded him modestly. 'I was younger then, and I was teamed up with Pee Wee, my big sorrel mare. She was the best roping horse around!'

Ben had been impressed nevertheless. He and Karina had sat talking for ages while Sandy and Kirstie had cleared away the remains of the supper.

Thinking back to the previous evening, Kirstie recalled some of the questions she'd stored up to ask Karina when she found the time. Like, whatever happened to Pee Wee the champion roping horse? And, how tough was it for a woman to make it in the macho rodeo world?

But for now, on the new wrangler's first morning at the ranch, there was a heap of work to be got through.

'Karina, I'd like you to stick around the ranch while Matt and I take the dude riders out to fetch in the calves,' Ben was explaining. His breath rose as clouds of steam into the freezing air. As yet, none of the guests were stirring, but it wouldn't be long before the corral was full of horses needing saddles and bridles, ready for the trek out along the trails.

The new hand nodded. 'OK, boss. What d'you want me to do?'

'You can work on the fence in Red Fox Meadow,' Ben explained. 'All the tools you need are stacked in the back of the Dodge. So why don't you drive out there as soon as you're ready?'

'Sure thing.' Dressed this morning in a thick checkered woollen jacket and a worn stetson, Karina pulled on her leather gloves and got ready for action.

'After the fence is fixed, I want you to drive out along Five Mile Creek Trail and clear a couple of logs felled by the last high winds.' Ben's list was workaday and hard.

Karina didn't object. 'Gotcha,' she said, stepping up into the tack-room to find the keys to the pick-up.

'How about you, Kirstie? You wanna ride out with us and bring in some calves?' Ben naturally included her in the more interesting side of the day's events.

But she shook her head. 'Nope. I guess I'll stick around and show Karina the trail.'

Ben nodded. 'OK, and when you're through with the logs, Matt wants us to work on a stall for

18

the little Appie. He figures we should keep her in the barn instead of out with the ramuda.'

Kirstie raised her eyebrows. Matt had promised Lauren that Lady Roseanne would get four-diamond treatment while she was away and Kirstie had guessed at the time that this would mean more work. Sure enough, Matt was behaving as if the Appaloosa mare would melt in the rain or blow away in the wind.

Ben grinned back but said nothing.

'Will it be OK for Karina and me to ride out along Five Mile Creek Trail instead of taking the truck?' Kirstie checked. 'I could take Lucky and Karina could ride Lady Roseanne. That way I show Karina the trail and the horse gets used to her new surroundings. When we get back, we'll fix up her stall real good.'

Laughing, Ben okayed the plan. 'Now I know why you volunteered to stick around!' He was still grinning and teasing when Karina emerged from the barn. 'No yakking when you should be working!' he warned, hoisting half a dozen head-collars on to his shoulder and heading out to the meadow. 'I know the way you gals are when you get together – all talk, talk, talk!'

* * *

Karina wielded a long-handled hammer and thumped a new fence post into position with four or five well-aimed blows. Then she took a roll of razor wire from the back of the Dodge and, hands protected by her thick gloves, she unravelled a length, snipped it with big steel cutters and stapled it firmly into position. When she'd finished, the new section of fence looked good and strong.

But not content with the specific task Ben had given her, Karina suggested that she and Kirstie went looking for other weak spots along the two hundred yard square perimeter.

Jumping into the truck beside her, Kirstie pointed out a stretch where the meadow fence crossed a shallow ditch which ran into the main creek. Young willows had shot up in the marshy ground during spring and summer, half hiding the razor wire. And it was clear that someone or something had tried to blunder its way through.

'We'll soon fix that.' Karina's sudden swerve towards the problem made the few horses who remained in the meadow kick up their heels and lope in the opposite direction.

Kirstie enjoyed the sight of Johnny Mohawk, Yukon and Rodeo Rocky racing across the frost covered field. But she didn't have long to admire the sight.

'C'mon, we gotta put our backs into cutting down these overgrown willows,' Karina urged, handing Kirstie the steel cutters and jumping down from the truck. 'I want to take a look at what's going on here.'

Soon the bendy willow saplings were gone and Karina was examining the area of running water and frozen red earth.

'See these prints?' Stooping low, Karina pointed out to Kirstie sets of paw prints criss-crossing the stream.

'Yeah. What do you reckon?' The prints were dog-like, showing the imprint of round pads and long claws.

The new wrangler studied them hard. 'Coyote,' she decided. 'More than one. Maybe a small pack of four or five.'

With a sharp intake of breath, Kirstie nodded to show that she agreed. 'We hear them at night,' she told Karina, 'but as a rule they don't come this close to the ranch.'

'Don't worry, they're only checking things out. They haven't strayed beyond the fence into the meadow.' Making doubly sure that the prints ended in the thicket of willow bushes, Karina reassured Kirstie about the horses in the meadow. 'Anyhow, a coyote won't take on a horse unless he's near to starving,' she pointed out. 'And you can bet your bottom dollar that there's easier food around this early in the winter.'

'So what are you saying? Do we or don't we make some attempt to keep them out?' Despite Karina's cheery tone, Kirstie couldn't help fearing for the likes of Jitterbug, who spooked easily, and Cadillac, who was also highly strung.

Karina stood up straight, adjusted her hat further back on her head, then thought things through. 'If it'll make you feel better, we could reinforce the fence right here with a couple of extra lengths of razor wire.' Before Kirstie had time to reply, she'd headed for the truck to begin the task.

Ten minutes later the job was done. 'Happy now?' Karina asked.

'Yeah, sorry. I've got this thing about coyotes when there are horses around.' If Kirstie was honest, the sleek, grey wolf-like creatures with the eerie howl scared the heck out of her.

'Well quit worrying. Even a coyote can't get through three rows of razor wire. And now that we've cleared the undergrowth, they won't risk being spotted out in the open at this end of the meadow.' Karina rightly pointed out that the fierce creatures liked the cover of the ponderosa pines growing on the slope at the far side of the meadow.

'I guess you think I'm a wimp,' Kirstie said as they stashed their tools in the Dodge and drove back to the ranch for lunch.

'Nope.' Grinning, Karina bumped and rattled the vehicle across the meadow. She waved at Hadley who was crossing the yard in the distance, giving a short laugh when the old-timer only shrugged in acknowledgement then turned away. 'What's his problem?' she murmured, pulling up the truck in a skid of frost and gravel. Then she jumped out and headed for the tack-room.

'D'you always move this fast?' Kirstie gasped, running to keep up. She was already finding that Karina raced through activities like an Olympic sprinter.

'Sure. Life's too short to pack everything in unless you do it at a lickety-split.' Like eating, for instance. Karina had already grabbed her sack-lunch, opened the paper bag and sunk her teeth into a wholewheat cheese and relish sandwich.

Kirstie leaned against the wind to force the tack-room door shut behind her. She noticed Cornbread shoot in out of the cold and straight away leap up on to the bench to attack her own parcel of food.

'Scat!' she told the kitten, scooping him off the table. He miaowed and snuggled close, reaching up to lick her face with his rough pink tongue. 'So tell me about the rodeo,' she invited Karina, keeping the kitten tucked under her arm and every now and then feeding him tidbits from her lunch.

'What's to tell?' Karina shrugged. She drank her coffee black without sugar and scalding-hot.

'What was your main event?' Eager to know more, Kirstie pressed Karina for details.

'First off, it was calf-roping. I was hooked on that since day one. I got a 98.2 second, ten-head record at the age of seventeen. Then I came back next year and smashed that with 95.3 seconds, which is about as good as it gets. So I got into team-roping and tried something new.'

'Wow!' Though Karina's tone was casual, Kirstie was majorly impressed. 'And which rodeo did you like competing in the best?'

'I guess my favourite was the Cheyenne,' Karina confessed. 'You get to hang out there for a week, and it's my type of show. They rope big calves and score 'em tough. That was a real challenge.'

Kirstie gave Karina a good close look. No more than five-foot-three, and still weighing only 130 pounds or less, it was hard to believe that she'd come out top in the rough, tough world of rodeo riding. 'Jeez,' she sighed enviously. 'I hope I get to do something like that by the time I'm seventeen!'

'Hey hold it!' Karina stood up and brushed crumbs of cheese to the floor. 'Did I also tell you that I broke my right ankle four times over and cracked this left elbow so bad the joint don't work properly no more?'

'Yeah, but—'

'No buts. Listen, honey, I didn't have no mom like Sandy to take care of me and put me through school. You count your blessings, believe me.'

25

'No mom?' Kirstie was curious. She abandoned the leftover sandwich and raced after Karina across the corral.

'My folks were killed in an airplane crash when I was eight years old,' Karina told her, thrusting a hay fork into her hands. 'Life's been pretty much a struggle for me ever since. And you listen good – hanging a couple of silver medals over your bed don't hardly make up for a cosy family life.'

Kirstie stared at the hay fork. 'I guess not,' she muttered. 'In fact, I guess cowboying and riding rodeo makes for a pretty tough life.'

'You bet.' Karina led her into the barn, chose a stall for Lady Roseanne and set to work with a broom.

'Especially for a woman?' Kirstie prompted.

'Yeah, you got it. The guys don't take easily to a gal doing the work, even now. When I was a kid it was worse. I entered the mixed male and female contests and got laughed out of every rodeo event in Colorado!'

'So you had to be better than them to prove the point?' Kirstie would love to have seen Karina in the ring, throwing a clean head catch, making two wraps and a hooey to tie the calf down.

'I guess,' Karina shrugged. She'd obviously talked enough about herself. 'It don't change much in spite of what they say,' she confided. 'Take Hadley and Matt last night. You could've cut the air with a knife when they saw Sandy had gone and hired a woman!'

'Hmm, Hadley,' Kirstie mumbled. 'Hadley's OK when you get to know him.'

'And what about your big brother?' As she swept straw and dust out of the stall, Karina paused to look Kirstie directly in the eye. 'What does he have against women?'

Kirstie blushed and stared back. 'His girlfriend just left for a trip to Europe. That put him in a bad mood, I guess. It's nothing against you personally, Karina. Honestly, believe me – that's the absolute truth!'

3

'The rock on the skyline to the west is Whiskey Rock, and that ridge to the north is Bear Hunt Overlook.' Pointing to the major landmarks surrounding the ranch, Kirstie helped Karina to get her bearings.

'What's the tall finger beyond the ridge?' Karina scanned the horizon, quietly taking in features of the landscape.

'Monument Rock. Then, way in the distance you can see Tigawon Mount, which is little sister to Eagle's Peak to the east.' To Kirstie, this wide open vista of mountain and forest was as familiar as the back of her hand. So she sat in the saddle, trying to figure out how it must be to see it all for the first time.

'Pretty,' Karina conceded, not wanting to go overboard with the compliments.

Which was something which the new wrangler had in common with Hadley, Kirstie realised with a smile. A cowgirl to the core, Karina didn't go in for long sentences and gushing emotions. She stuck to the practical and kept her thoughts to herself.

'Name me some other trails,' she said, reining Lady Roseanne away from the lookout point and heading back down towards Five Mile Creek.

'Coyote Trail takes you up a forest track,' Kirstie replied, having to hurry as usual. Her palomino, Lucky, picked his way nimbly between rocks and low bushes, sliding easily across stretches of loose dirt, keeping his balance as he went. 'Then there's Bear Hunt Trail, and Eagle's Peak Trail for more advanced riders—'

'What's your favourite?' Karina cut in. They were still looking for the stretch of trail where

29

fallen trees had blocked the way. As they rode upstream, the creek grew narrower and the current faster.

'This one's pretty neat,' Kirstie admitted. 'If you ride deeper into the mountains, you come to Crystal Falls. They're beautiful. And eventually you reach Eden Lake. It's above the snow line, so the water stays frozen most of the year.'

'Hmm. How about native wildlife?' Riding Roseanne close to the edge of the creek, Karina demanded still more facts.

Kirstie promptly provided a long list. 'Coyote, mountain lion, bobcat, black bear, red fox, grey fox, mule deer, skunk, raccoon, sometimes elk and bighorn . . .'

'Whoa!' Karina grinned.

'You did ask!'

'Sure. But look, these must be the trees that are causing the problem.' Pointing to three pines felled during the high wind, Karina jumped down from Roseanne's saddle.

The trees were each about twenty feet high and eighteen inches across at the base. This meant they were too heavy to lift, Kirstie realised, and she began to wish that she and Karina had chosen the more practical option of driving out with a truck-load of tools.

But the wrangler wasn't deterred by the size and dead weight. 'That must've been some wind,' she commented, reaching for a length of rope which she'd coiled round Roseanne's saddle horn.

The pines had fallen at odd angles, their branches tangling together as they crashed to the ground, so Karina's first job was to single out the one that could most easily be moved. She soon did this, then tied one end of the rope round its trunk. Taking the other end, she secured it to her saddle horn.

Kirstie watched with interest. 'I never had Lady Roseanne figured as a workhorse,' she commented, noting the Appie's slight frame. 'She's a little dainty for the heavy stuff, don't you think?'

Karina agreed. 'Which is why I need you to grab a hold of the trunk and help to lift it while Roseanne pulls,' she explained. Without giving Kirstie time to argue, she made her take up position and get ready to heave.

Kirstie awaited her orders. The sweet, strong smell of pine resin filled her nostrils and the sharp needles pricked her face and arms. Meanwhile, Karina stood by the Appaloosa's head, inching her away from the trees until the rope was taut and the horse took the strain.

'Ready?' Karina called over her shoulder.

'Yep. Ready as I'll ever be!' Still not convinced that this would work, Kirstie braced herself.

'Lift!' Karina yelled as she clicked her tongue and flicked Roseanne's hindquarters with the loose end of one rein.

The gutsy little horse strained forwards. Branches of the tangled trees snapped as

Roseanne took one step, then two. Kirstie hauled with all her might. The top tree trunk was moving after all.

'Walk on!' Karina urged Lady Roseanne. 'Good girl; you can do it!'

The mare pulled until her eyes bulged and her breath came in heavy gasps. Her sides heaved and she stumbled as she put every ounce of effort into the task.

'Jeez, am I glad Matt can't see this!' Kirstie muttered as finally she was able to shove the tree clear. 'Y'know, Karina – next time I reckon we ought to use Lucky to do the lumberjack work.'

'Yeah, maybe he packs a little more muscle,' the wrangler agreed. 'But good job, Roseanne!' Patting the Appie before she released the rope from her saddle horn and led her to the spot where Lucky stood, Karina made it clear that she appreciated the mare's help. 'You're not just a pretty little thing,' she told her. 'You're a good worker too.'

The Appaloosa lowered her head and breathed in deep. Then she gave Karina's hand a gentle nudge.

'Yeah!' Coming up to prepare her palomino

for his log-shifting session, Kirstie joined in the praise. 'You're a horse in a million!'

Good-tempered and beautiful, plucky and gracious, Lady Roseanne sure stood out from the crowd.

'What kept you?' Matt demanded the moment they got back.

He stood, legs wide apart, arms folded at the gate to the corral. Over in the holding-pen by the creek, five scared calves hollered for their mothers.

His sharp question broke Kirstie's satisfied mood. 'It turned out to be a tough job,' she told him. 'They were whole trees we had to shift back there – not just any old logs!'

She and Karina had achieved what had looked impossible at first glance and they were pleased with the way things had gone. They'd given each other a high-five before remounting their horses and hightailing it back to the ranch. Sure, it was already growing dusk and the temperature was dropping way down for a second night running, but still there was no need for her brother to come over heavy.

Matt sniffed and strode across to take Lady Roseanne's reins from Karina before she'd even dismounted. 'This mare is all lathered up,' he snapped. 'It looks to me like she's been ridden too hard.'

Karina frowned at the criticism. 'You'd rather we'd come back slower and still been out there after dark?'

Ignoring her, Matt led Roseanne towards the barn. 'What's this cut on her hock?' he demanded, once they were all inside.

Trust Matt to spot a graze half an inch long on the Appie's front leg. Kirstie could only just see it in the glare of the electric light. It must have happened without them even noticing it and obviously wasn't causing the mare the least little problem.

'You want me to clean it up and apply an anti-septic cream?' Karina volunteered. She'd obviously decided to bite her lip rather than challenge the boss's son any further.

'Leave it to me,' he said ungraciously, leading Roseanne into her specially cleaned and prepared stall. There was hay in the manger, water in her bucket and a heap of squeaky-clean straw for her to bed down on.

Kirstie saw Karina's frown deepen. 'I'll go check in with Ben,' she muttered. By the time Kirstie had unsaddled Lucky and was carrying his tack out into the corral, Karina was ready to make a quick exit from the barn.

'I thought you said your brother had nothing against me,' she grunted under her breath.

Kirstie sighed and admitted Matt had been out of line.

Karina strode ahead of her towards the tack-room. 'You bet he was,' she agreed. 'Way out of line. And if that isn't a clear example of him holding a grudge against me personally, I sure wouldn't like to see what is!'

'Call it a personality clash,' Sandy told Kirstie, after more examples of Matt's impatience with Karina had come to light.

A week had passed, during which Karina had leaned over backwards to do everything right and Matt had been equally set on finding fault. According to him, Karina didn't clean tack thoroughly, pitch hay with the right fork, or even scoop poop with the correct spade.

Now, on Saturday morning, when Matt had left early to drive into San Luis, Kirstie grabbed the chance to relay the growing problem to her mom.

The two of them were out in Red Fox Meadow, selecting horses to trailer to winter pasture in Aspen Park. Without wanting to come down too hard on her brother, Kirstie had felt it right to warn Sandy that Karina might not be able to take much more unfair criticism.

'Matt and Karina are too alike, that's the problem,' Sandy said, cutting Crazy Horse out from the herd. The old gelding needed to be sent to the kinder climate of the Park, where his creaky bones wouldn't suffer so badly from the frost and snow. And if Crazy Horse went, then Cadillac must go along in the trailer with him, since the two were inseparable.

'How d'you figure that?' Kirstie asked, going after Matt's thoroughbred.

'They're both pig-headed – period!' Sandy told it like it was. 'Karina was always made that way, even when we were kids. She had her own style of doing things and no one could tell her different. In a sense, that's what makes her so good in the rodeo ring. You need an ornery streak to get in there and compete.'

'But why should that get under Matt's skin?' Slipping a headcollar on Cadillac, Kirstie joined her mom. 'If they're both stubborn, how come he doesn't appreciate that in her?'

'Matt's got stuff on his mind, that's why,' Sandy replied.

'Didn't he hear from Lauren yet?'

'Nope. Not a single phone call, e-mail, fax – nothing. He checks at least five times per day.'

'So, tell him not to take it out on Karina.' Kirstie pointed out the injustice as they led the two horses out of the meadow. Cadillac and Crazy Horse were the last to be trailered, joining Jitterbug, Hollywood Princess and Gunsmoke in the trip to winter pasture.

Sandy sighed. 'Yeah, I know – it ain't fair. But Karina can handle it. She expects a tough ride whenever she starts out in a new job, and so far she's come out on top.'

They had to drop the subject when they reached the yard because Karina herself was waiting by the long silver trailer to load the last two horses.

Seeing what lay ahead, Cadillac protested,

beginning to pull at his lead-rope and dig in his heels. Legs splayed wide, the nervous thoroughbred declined to enter the trailer.

So Kirstie went ahead with Crazy Horse. The plain old light sorrel gelding plodded on up the ramp without a murmur and was soon tied alongside Hollywood Princess. 'C'mon, Cadillac!' Kirstie coaxed, knowing this would do the trick. 'You don't wanna be left all on your ownsome, do you?'

Sure enough, a panicky look came into Cadillac's eyes. He glanced up into the dark trailer and gave a low whinny. Then he trotted smartly after his pal, almost dragging Sandy with him.

'Good job!' Quickly Karina raised the ramp and bolted it into place. This was the second run today and they all expected the operation to pass off smoothly. 'You wanna come or stay?' she checked with Kirstie.

'Come!' Kirstie had saved this second trip to ask Karina a hundred questions about Pee Wee, the wonder horse. Trapped in the cab during the fifty minute drive, the reluctant rodeo star would have no choice but to answer.

So they set off up the drive and on to the Shelf-

Road, with the half dozen horses shifting uneasily in the back. Sandy had waved them off and gone inside to catch up with paperwork, trusting Karina with the valuable cargo.

Ten minutes along the winding dirt track, Kirstie still hadn't squeezed a single answer out of Karina about her glory days.

'Let me focus on my driving,' she urged. 'These bends don't leave much room for manoeuvre.'

It was true that the Shelf-Road needed Karina's full concentration, dropping steeply away on one side and cut tight into sheer cliffs on the other. Long stretches of ice on the loose surface made for a double hazard and with a load of restless horses swaying and stamping in the back, the journey was sometimes touch and go.

However they made it eventually on to an official National Forest road, where the going was flatter and easier. Karina relaxed and began to power along at forty miles per hour, giving grudging replies to Kirstie's eager questions.

'How old were you when you bought Pee Wee?'

'I was thirteen. I didn't buy her exactly. She belonged to Mr Jameson, a guy I cleaned house for at the weekends. Before that I spent a couple of summers riding the hair off the back of an ornery Shetland pony. I didn't have no saddle or nothing, but I was kinda undersized and the Shetland carried me no problem.

'Mr Jameson, he saw how crazy I was to ride rodeo, so he kinda loaned me a saddle and a mount – a bay mare with a wall eye. That was when Pee Wee and me became a team.'

'Jeez!' Once more the romance of it all struck Kirstie. But before she had time to jump in with a second question, she felt Karina slam on the brake.

The trailer skidded and slewed sideways towards the middle of the road. It stopped just in time to avoid a car which appeared round a bend, driving at speed.

The car too slid to a halt at a dangerous angle, only feet away from the trailer.

'Matt!' Straightaway Kirstie recognised the beaten-up car and its young, dark-haired driver. She jumped down from the cab while Karina ran to the back of the trailer to check that the horses had survived the sudden stop. 'How come you were driving so fast?'

He got out with a face like thunder. 'Me?' he

demanded. 'What was that crazy female doin',
throwin' the trailer round a bend like that?'

'She wasn't . . . it was . . .' Kirstie's breathless
sentence trailed off as Matt strode across to bawl
Karina out.

'You tryin' to kill those horses, or somethin'?'

'Nope,' she said evenly, stepping down from
the back fender now that she was satisfied that
her passengers hadn't suffered any damage.

'It sure looked like it to me. You were doing
sixty back there!'

'Yeah? Well, let's be thankful no one got hurt.'
Her mouth set in a grim line, Karina was ready
to back off and keep on driving to the Park.

'No thanks to you!' Matt acted like he was
determined to grind her face into the dirt. 'You
sure you've got a licence to drive a trailer this
size, or do I need to double check that with the
central issuing office?'

'That'd be your choice,' she shrugged. Then
she showed a flash of temper. 'All I can say is
that I've been driving trucks through fifteen states
since before you were born, Matt Scott. And
nobody, but nobody ever questioned my
qualifications to date!'

The anger in her voice took Matt by surprise. He backed off, allowing her space to squeeze through between him and the trailer. Watching her climb back into the cab, he went on muttering under his breath.

'Oh great, Matt!' Kirstie said through gritted teeth. 'You almost cause a serious accident and what do you do? You blame the other guy!'

'You comin', Kirstie?' Karina called impatiently.

'Yeah!' she yelled back. She left her brother with a parting shot. 'You're lucky Karina's reactions were so fast. If she hadn't braked when she did, right now you'd probably be lying stone cold dead in a twisted heap of metal. You remember that before you go shooting your mouth off next time!'

Somehow the pleasure of setting the horses loose in Aspen Park drained away the frustration of the episode with Matt.

Kirstie and Karina sat astride the fence watching Cadillac race away up the gentle slope, followed by clumsy old Crazy Horse. Next to emerge from the trailer was Hollywood Princess. The Albino horse sniffed the autumn air, then took to her heels in a different direction, towards a clear blue lake edged with aspens.

'Hey, Jitterbug!' Kirstie murmured to encourage the shy sorrel as she poked her nose out of the trailer. 'This is your winter home. Do you like it?'

Jitterbug trod gingerly down the ramp, danced sideways, crow-hopped, then took off after Cadillac and Crazy Horse. Last came Gunsmoke with his weird, shuffling, Paso Fino gait – half walk, half trot. He too tested the air, picked up the smell of fallen leaves, wet grass, a distant scent of woodsmoke. And off he went at a smooth lope to join Hollywood Princess.

'Hmm.' Giving a grunt of satisfaction, Karina jumped down from the fence. 'Say what you like about the problems of the job, this sure is pretty country and a mighty fine way for a gal to live!'

4

'I tell you, Mom – Karina was driving that trailer
down the Forest Road like she was on a Formula
One racetrack!'

Kirstie had got back to the house from Aspen
Park to find Matt hacking away at Karina's good
name. Why couldn't he give it a rest? And how
come he always exaggerated?

Sandy listened calmly. 'That's a serious charge,'
she warned him. 'In my book, anyone who drives
recklessly with five horses in the back of the
trailer is in deep trouble.'

Matt stuck to his guns – even though he registered Kirstie's entrance and the way she flung her hat down on the kitchen table in pure disgust. 'Believe me, she almost caused a bad accident.'

'So how fast was she going?' Facts were what mattered to Sandy.

'Sixty miles per hour, plus some. She was raising dirt and skidding across the track when I came round the bend!'

'No way,' Kirstie cut in. 'We were doing forty on a straight stretch. It was you, Matt, who almost caused the accident and you know it!'

Sandy swung round to face her. 'Yeah, you were there. You're sure none of the horses were hurt?'

Nodding, Kirstie glowered at her brother. 'I told you not to go shooting your mouth off. What is it with you?'

Cornered, Matt grew angrier still. 'Yeah, that's right. Stick up for your cowgirl hero, why don't you?'

'I'm only saying what's true,' she insisted. 'You were driving back from town in a bad mood and you were the one who was doing sixty miles per hour. So if I were you, Matt Scott, I'd cool it!'

'Listen, why don't you both calm down?' Sandy broke in. 'Luckily, it sounds like no one got hurt. And, son – go easy on Karina, huh?'

About to come back at her with some smart reply, Matt thought better of it. 'Yes, ma'am,' he muttered, hoisting his own hat from the hook by the door and stamping out.

'Hothead,' Sandy sighed, shaking her head and disappearing upstairs. 'Just like his dad.'

Kirstie and Matt's father had left the family for another woman when Kirstie was nine years old. Mention of him still brought a sharp pain to her heart and a twist to her stomach. She remembered his quick temper, but also his fun-loving streak – the games of baseball he would set up in their small back yard in Denver, his loud laugh when she used to swing the bat and miss.

So she felt down as she sat alone at the kitchen table and picked at her lunch. For once, she couldn't summon much enthusiasm for going out to work in the corral with Ben – who was stacking hay bales in the barn. Instead, she decided to wander out to the meadow and spend some quiet time with the horses who had been chosen because of their hardiness to remain at the ranch all through the long winter to come.

The wind cut through the denim jacket that she'd flung on as she left the house. Heavy clouds over Eagle's Peak threatened the first snowfall of the season.

'Lucky we brought in all the calves for branding and pushed them out back with their mothers!' Ben called, as he crossed the corral. 'Hey, how about you put some miles on Lady Roseanne this afternoon if you've got nothing more important lined up?'

'Wow, yeah!' The idea lifted her straight away. 'Is she out in the meadow or in her stall?'

'Meadow,' the head wrangler answered. 'She made friends with Joe while you and Karina were out this morning. Two Appaloosas against the rest!'

Kirstie smiled at the odd couple. Refined and gentle Lady Roseanne with muscleman Navaho Joe. Joe was the half-wild Appie whom they'd found wandering in the mountains the previous winter. They'd brought him in and worked with him, but he was still a handful.

Yet, true enough, she found the two horses in

a corner of the meadow, fending off the rest of the ramuda and hogging a manger of hay all to themselves. Joe bullied and nipped all-comers, snatching mouthfuls of alfalfa in between times, while Roseanne picked and nibbled daintily.

'Hey, Joe!' Kirstie approached quietly. 'You gonna let me take your new buddy out on the trail?'

Navaho Joe flicked his ears and snorted. Then he backed away to let Kirstie by.

'Smart move,' she told him. 'Didn't I always say that Appies are way out ahead in the brain department?'

Joe stamped his agreement, abandoning the manger to Rodeo Rocky and following Kirstie and Roseanne towards the gate.

'Don't worry, she'll be back!' Kirstie promised him with a laugh. 'I only plan to ride out to Angel Rock and get her back home before it snows!'

Angel Rock was a secret, magical place. No guests were ever taken there and it was so off the beaten track that only deer and other woodland animals ever discovered it.

Now, in mid-fall, the last aspen leaves were

falling and icicles had already formed on the series of small waterfalls which slid over ledges from the towering rock which gave the spot its name. Later in the afternoon, when the sun finally got around to shining in this deserted spot, Kirstie knew that the icicles would melt and free up the delicate green ferns that grew at the water's edge. But for now, all was shaded and covered in stiff white frost.

The Angel gazed down silently at Lady Roseanne and her rider.

People called this rock the Angel because, looked at sideways on, it had the shape of a Christmas angel on top of the tree. Kirstie could see it clearly – the half-raised wings, the praying hands. And she wanted to share it with the little Appie, who as it happened seemed to appreciate the silent beauty of the place.

Even when a mule deer broke through some thick thorn bushes and leaped across the clearing, at first Roseanne didn't flinch.

'I wonder what spooked him?' Kirstie murmured, watching the white hindquarters of the buck disappear down a steep slope. She thought no more of it as she reined Roseanne to the right and turned for home.

But whatever it was that had alarmed the deer eventually affected the mare too. Instead of setting off gently down the wooded hillside, she laid back her ears and braced all four legs, ready to buck.

'Easy!' Kirstie breathed, tightening the reins to gain control.

Roseanne tossed her head to resist the rein. She crow-hopped on stiff legs, rounding her back to jolt Kirstie out of the saddle.

Kirstie leaned back and sat down hard. What was going on here to make the normally placid and co-operative Appaloosa suddenly cut up rough?

Another two deer shot out from the undergrowth, bounding on their spindly legs over rocks not six feet from where Kirstie battled to calm Lady Roseanne. The horse reared up on her hindlegs, throwing her rider even further back in the deep saddle.

'Jeez!' Kirstie pitched her weight forward and brought Roseanne down on to all fours. It needed split-second timing to stay on and keep her mount from sliding, out of control, down the slope.

Now Kirstie could hear sounds of heavier animals crashing out of sight in the brittle undergrowth. For sure this was what had upset the deer and disturbed the mare. But she was in no position to stick around and investigate. Lady Roseanne had it in her head to take off after the deer, and once twelve hundred pounds of horse muscle had reached such a decision, there was no way a rider weighing a mere hundred and fifteen could stop her.

Roseanne gave a high whinny and set off at a bumpy trot, crashing through bushes and stumbling against boulders. Kirstie gripped the saddle horn and hung on. She ducked low branches, leaned away from solid tree trunks, feeling the saddle slip sideways and desperately trying to right it again as Roseanne blundered on.

At last they came to level ground. The deer were long gone and the sounds of the mysterious animals in the undergrowth had died away. At least Kirstie and Roseanne were not being pursued. Kirstie breathed a sigh of relief as she managed to pull her horse up and re-establish control.

But still the Appie cast cautious looks over her shoulder and stayed on the alert.

'Yeah, I know, you're all shook up,' Kirstie muttered, quickly dismounting to tighten the cinch. 'You wish Joe was around to keep you company and tell you everything's OK. But you've just gotta cowboy up all by yourself and be a big, brave girl!'

Kirstie had some sympathy for the way Roseanne had acted. After all, she was sure that Lauren would never have ridden her out in such wild country, and the mare wasn't used to the challenge. And those bush sounds had been pretty scary – something big and heavy had made them. On top of that, the Appie's acute sense of smell would have picked up a scent that signalled danger. All in all Kirstie felt they'd done well to get out in one piece.

But it wasn't over yet. After the mystery animal came the snow.

Earlier than forecast, big white flakes began to fall. Whipped by the wind, they flew into Kirstie and Roseanne's faces and settled on the trail ahead. Soon the whole landscape was dusted with an unfamiliar white.

'That's all we need!' Kirstie groaned. The ranch was an hour's ride from here, and no way was she dressed for these extreme conditions. She had no gloves, no slicker to protect herself from the snow. And poor Roseanne grew quickly miserable, lowering her head and plodding doggedly into the whirling flakes.

Worse still, after ten minutes or so, the going underfoot grew slippery and uncertain. Snow drifted into the holes and ridges worn into the track by summer rains. The hidden hazards caught the Appie by surprise, making her stumble and almost fall. Twice she went down on to her knees, recovering just in time to stop Kirstie from diving head first over her withers.

'Please stop!' Kirstie prayed in vain for the freezing flakes to ease. Her fingers were numb with cold, her face frozen into a deep frown. By the time the ranch came into view in the valley below, she was almost rigid in the saddle.

But then, to her relief, she spied a horse and rider heading out to meet them. Blurred at first because of the flurries of snow and the grim darkness cast by the low clouds, Kirstie was eventually able to make out Karina and Navaho Joe.

'What kept you?' Karina yelled, urging Joe into a lope in spite of the conditions. 'You had us all treading on eggshells back there. Your mom was ready to call in the mountain rescue team!'

Jaw juddering with cold, Kirstie tried to reply. 'Am I in trouble?'

'You bet!' Coming up alongside, Karina took hold of Kirstie's reins. 'Matt's tearing his hair out over Lady Roseanne. He swears he's never gonna let any of us lay hands on her ever again!'

'Huh!' That was how much he cared. All he thought about when Kirstie was lost in a snowstorm was Lauren's precious horse!

Karina saw how close to the edge Kirstie was. 'That'll teach you to ride out in a thin jacket and no gloves! How are your feet?'

'Like blocks of ice.'

'C'mon, let's get you home. I'll dally Roseanne along after Joe; that should be the quickest method.'

Leading the way at a smart trot, Karina and Navaho Joe got Kirstie and Lady Roseanne back to the ranch in double-quick time. They were greeted by a huddle of people standing in the house porch: Sandy dressed in scarf and thick leather jacket, Ben braving the weather in worn work denims, Hadley in his long yellow slicker.

'Thank goodness!' Sandy came out into the yard to help Kirstie out of the saddle. 'Next time you head out alone, you take a two-way radio, remember!'

Nodding, Kirstie shed two inches of snow from the brim of her stetson. She patted Roseanne's neck with frozen fingers, then shook out the icy chunks from her long white mane.

'Where's Matt?' she muttered. If she was going to get it in the neck from her angry brother, she'd rather have it over with here and now.

'He's on the phone,' Sandy told her. 'It just so happens that Lauren called at last. I say, lucky for you that he has a major distraction!'

'Quick, give me Roseanne's reins.' Karina moved fast to get the mare into the barn and out of sight before Matt came off the phone.

Fumbling and stumbling on to the porch, Kirstie did as she was told.

'Don't worry about a thing, OK?' Karina reassured them. 'I'll take care of the Appie and

56

bed her down in the barn for the night. You all just get inside the house and let Matt know that it worked out fine!'

After the phone call from Lauren in Europe, Matt acted like a different person.

'She's in London,' he told Sandy and Kirstie, hardly stopping to check the details of what had gone on for Kirstie and Lady Roseanne when the snow had suddenly set in. 'She's seen the British Houses of Parliament and the Tower. Oh yeah, and that neat thing they do at the gates of Buckingham Palace – the Changing of the Guard.'

The big log fire, the hot chocolate, her brother easing off at last and becoming more like a normal human being again, lulled Kirstie into deciding that an early night and a fresh start come tomorrow morning was the best thing she could do after her freezing adventure.

So, thawed out and sleepy, she climbed the stairs to bed, waking soon after dawn to a warm, blue-skied Sunday.

Never ask what the weather is gonna do in Colorado! Kirstie grinned to herself as she scrambled into clean jeans and a sweatshirt. There was no predicting the sudden changes. Instead, you just went with the flow.

Refreshed by her long sleep, she was eager to get out to the barn to check up on how Lady Roseanne had survived their adventure. She would muck her out and fill her manger with the best alfalfa, promise her a morning out in Red Fox Meadow with her best buddy, Navaho Joe, as long as Matt gave his seal of approval.

The bluest of blue skies greeted her as she swung out of the house. The white summit of Eagle's Peak glittered in the early morning sun and two jays swooped down from the barn roof. This was the time Kirstie most enjoyed – the quiet, still start of a brand new day.

Her footsteps crunched over crisp snow which had drifted to a depth of twelve inches against the door of the barn. She had to scrape the snow away with the heel of her boot before she could open the door. Then once inside the barn, she stopped to kick off the compacted snow.

From the far end of the central aisle Lady Roseanne acknowledged Kirstie's arrival with a low whinny.

'Yep, it's breakfast time!' Kirstie called cheerily, pausing again to pick up a fork and bucket for the business of mucking out the stall. Her eyes took a few seconds to get used to the dark interior, so she trod carefully past the wooden box containing old stirrups in need of repair and a tall grain barrel full of winter feed supplement. 'Hey!' she called, expecting to see Roseanne's white head appear at the stall door. 'Didn't you hear me say the word "breakfast"?'

It was only when she reached Roseanne's luxury quarters that she understood why the horse hadn't responded. The sight there made Kirstie gasp and slam down the bucket and fork.

The Appie was lying on her side, legs folded under her. Her sides were heaving in and out, and she was only able to raise her head feebly from the blood-stained straw.

'Oh Jeez, what happened?' Kirstie cried. She felt a surge of panic rise in her throat as she slammed open the bolt and rushed into the stall.

Roseanne's head sank back to the ground. Kirstie crouched beside her and found that her legs and neck were covered in dozens of cuts and abrasions. One cut in particular stretched four inches across her shoulder and had gone deep into the flesh. The wound still bled heavily, seeping into the bedding.

'Did I do this?' For a moment, Kirstie had the crazy idea that Roseanne's injuries had been caused by their wild slide down the hill from Angel Rock the day before.

Then common sense told her no – she would have known it at the time. Roseanne would have had to limp home with a cut this deep and Karina would have spotted it as she'd brought her into the barn.

So it must have happened later – some time during the night.

In any case, Kirstie had to act fast. 'Stay still,' she murmured to Roseanne, who was again trying to raise her head. Gently she stroked her cheek to make her lie down. Then she ran to grab an empty grain sack, fold it and pad it against the deepest cut, tying it into place with a lead-rope round her neck and under her belly. This temporary dressing might at least stop the flow of blood.

'I'll fetch help!' she promised, scrambling to her feet. She raced out of the barn into the daylight, saw that the tack-room door stood open and made straight for it.

Inside she found Karina stirring a big tub of creosote paint with a long stick. Sunday was fence painting day, apparently.

But Kirstie pulled the wrangler away from the task, hardly able to speak. 'It's Roseanne!' she gasped, dragging Karina out into the open, spying Matt step out of the house on to the porch as they went.

Karina quickly tuned in to the urgency of the situation and outsprinted Kirstie down the central aisle of the barn. She was down on her knees, lifting Kirstie's crude dressing and examining the worst wound, when Matt broke in on them.

'What the heck . . . !' he yelled, his face white, his voice almost breaking down. Then he quickly got a hold on his sense of shock and went into vet mode. 'Fetch my first-aid kit from the tack-room!' he yelled at Kirstie. 'Get out of the way, Karina. Didn't you do enough damage already?'

Karina overbalanced against the wall of the stall as Matt shoved her to one side. 'Come again?' she muttered.

'I said, this is all down to you and you know it!' Matt was replacing the pad of sacking and pressing hard on the wound. 'You stalled Roseanne last night and you managed to completely overlook the fact that the horse was injured!'

'No way!' Karina got slowly to her feet. This time she was determined to have her say. 'You're talking garbage here and you know it!'

Matt flung a second order at Kirstie. 'Fetch Mom. Tell her Karina left Roseanne to bleed to death!'

'Matt . . .' Kirstie protested.

'You tell me how else this could happen. Think about it!'

'These cuts happened since suppertime yesterday,' Karina tried to point out. 'This is fresh blood. Besides, it looks to me like they could be self-inflicted by the mare lashing out against the sides of her stall.'

But Matt refused to listen. As Lady Roseanne's blood soaked through the pad and stained his hands red, he glared up at Karina.

'You take back what you said about me leaving her to bleed to death,' she insisted.

'No way. That's exactly how it happened!'

'I'll fetch Mom!' It was the only way Kirstie could think of to settle the fight and focus the attention on the injured horse.

She was on the point of running to the house, when Karina stopped her.

'Forget it,' she said, her voice deadly calm. 'No contest, Matt. You're the boss's son, so you win.'

'What do you mean?' Kirstie gasped.

'I mean I quit,' Karina told her, letting her shoulders sag and a look of defeat appear in her eyes. 'I'm outta here – period!'

5

The crucial thing was to get Lady Roseanne back on her feet. A horse that had gone down was two-thirds of the way to defeat, Kirstie knew. In the wild, it wouldn't have been long before predators moved in.

So she, Matt and their mom had to work fast. While Matt kept up the pressure on the main wound, Kirstie was given the task of cleaning the minor cuts, dabbing at them with antibacterial soap and clipping back the hair until she was sure the skin would heal properly. Meanwhile, Sandy asked Matt about bringing in vet, Glen Woodford to give a blood transfusion.

'No need,' Matt assured her, using equipment from his bag to suture the wound.

'It sure looks like she lost a lot.' Sandy's voice was deeply concerned, but she was ready to trust her son's opinion.

'Yeah, that's true,' he acknowledged. 'She severed an artery, so the blood pumps out fast.'

Kirstie winced then went on cleaning up the small cuts and abrasions.

'But it probably looks worse than it is. And now that I got the sutures in place and the bleeding's under control, I reckon we're gonna be OK.' Matt stood up and looked round the stall. 'Fill up the water bucket,' he told Kirstie. 'She'll need lots of replacement fluid.'

'What about a shot of antibiotics?' Still worried about the cuts becoming infected, Kirstie hassled him.

'Yeah, yeah. I already got that. We also need to check that her tetanus immunization is up to date. I guess I should call Lauren's parents to find out. And we keep at these cuts with the Nitrofurazone ointment over the next couple of days. Plus 25 cc of Procaine twice a day.' Thorough as ever, Matt covered every angle.

'What d'you reckon – do we bandage over the top of the sutures?' Sandy was on her knees, trying to urge Roseanne to stand. The mare responded to her voice by shifting her weight gingerly on to her knees, getting ready to push upwards.

'Uh-huh.' Matt's answer was firm. 'We leave this one open so it heals from the inside out. Otherwise we get abscesses. Kirstie, you gotta wash the area every day to remove the scab, then I can flush it with antiseptic. This is gonna take a long time to clear up.'

Say what you liked about Matt's short fuse, Kirstie thought, at times like this you could trust him completely. She might even go as far as to admit that he was well on the way to being an excellent vet.

Watching her mom gently encourage Lady Roseanne to stand, she began to relax. The mare was going to survive. In fact, she was eager to get to her feet and duck her nose into the water bucket, thirstily sucking up liquid and gulping it down.

Another good sign was that when she'd finished drinking, she raised her head, turned and gave a call towards the ramuda. The answering high whinny seemed to pep her up and make her experiment with a couple of wobbly steps across the stall.

'Would you listen to Navaho Joe!' Kirstie allowed herself a brief grin at the raucous Appaloosa out in the meadow. Joe seemed to be tuned in to what had happened and be urging Roseanne towards a speedy recovery.

'I still want to know how she ended up in this pitiful state,' Sandy said more thoughtfully, bringing Kirstie back to earth with a bump. 'I don't like mysteries. They make me feel out of control, as if the whole thing could occur over again.'

Kirstie saw the frown lines form on Matt's face. 'This kind of thing only happens when you employ the wrong staff,' he muttered.

Sandy stared at him. 'Surely to goodness you're not claiming that Karina is behind this?'

'It's the old story,' Kirstie explained. 'Matt's obsessed with Lady Roseanne because she belongs to Lauren and he promised to take good care of her. So he's all off-balance and he needs to find somone to blame, even for the least little thing—' She stopped abruptly as she realised that both her mom and Matt had turned to stare at her instead. 'It's true!' she insisted. 'Matt's developed this thing about Karina because, deep inside, he's scared he's gonna lose Lauren!'

Actually, she surprised herself by what she came out with. It was heavy stuff. But she was convinced she was right. 'On top of which, Matt's so pig-headed, he can't believe a woman can do a wrangler's job as well as a guy!'

'But Karina's living proof that the opposite is true,' Sandy pointed out. She lingered by Lady Roseanne's side, making sure that the injured Appie was strong enough to feed and water. 'Y'know, when I heard she was looking for a new position and I decided to employ her, it never even crossed my mind that it could be a problem.'

'Yeah, well don't listen to Kirstie,' Matt protested, clearing away his instruments, then picking straw out of the tops of his boots – anything to avoid looking Sandy in the eye. 'I didn't object to Karina because she was a woman. That wasn't it at all.'

'Oh no? Did you see his face when Karina first walked through the door?' Kirstie insisted. 'Are you telling me that he was fair and even-handed to her? The fact is, he was as bad as Hadley. The two of them never even gave her a chance!'

Sandy took in both sides of the argument. 'What's this about "was" and "didn't"?' she asked. 'Why the past tense?'

There was silence in the barn. Kirstie too dropped her gaze.

'C'mon, what didn't you tell me?' Their mom pressed for an answer.

Matt mumbled under his breath and began to walk away.

'Kirstie, what happened?' Sandy demanded, stepping forward to bar her exit.

'Karina quit,' she mumbled.

'What?' Her mom couldn't believe her ears.

'She quit,' Kirstie repeated. 'If you really want to know, Matt drove her to it. Karina's leaving Half-Moon Ranch because of him, OK!'

When Karina made up her mind, she acted fast.

She'd already been to the bunkhouse, packed her bag and was out in the yard asking Hadley for a lift into town by the time Sandy had caught up with events.

'What d'you mean, you quit?' Hadley acted like he hadn't heard right, cupping one hand to his ear and getting Karina to repeat what she'd said.

'I mean I can see when the writing's on the wall. No way can folks around here accept me for what I am. So instead of fighting it I guess I'll be on my way.'

'Hmm.' The old-timer sniffed. 'And you want me to drive you into San Luis?'

Karina nodded. 'I hear you're heading that way anyhow.' By this time she'd caught sight of Sandy and Kirstie standing indecisively in the barn doorway. 'Listen, Hadley, do I get the ride or not?'

'Huh,' he grouched. 'I didn't have you down as a quitter.' He too had seen his boss and Kirstie but his body language seemed to warn them to keep their distance. He turned his back and leaned against the roof of his pick-up.

'This isn't quitting, as in "quitting"!' Karina protested. 'I don't give in easy, if that's what you mean. But anyone with a grain of sense can see I'm not welcome round here.'

Hadley shrugged. 'Yeah well. It looks like quittin' to me.'

Exasperated, Karina picked her bag up, ready to walk away. 'Forget the ride. I'll make my own way.'

Sandy was about to run after her when suddenly Karina stopped of her own accord.

'You reckon I'm wimpin' out?' she asked the old man.

Hadley tipped his hat on to the back of his head. 'Yes, ma'am,' he growled.

'So you think I should stick around?'

71

The same shrug as before. The same gruff, non-committal growl.

Karina retraced her steps. 'Put it this way – if you were me, you'd stay?'

Hadley sniffed. 'I never quit a place on account of some other guy takin' a dislike to me and that's the truth.'

'But did you ever get accused of stuff you didn't do?' Karina glanced over her shoulder at Sandy and Kirstie, aware that it was make her mind up time. If she didn't walk away now, she never would.

'You mean Matt?' Hadley asked, swatting the air as if a fly was bothering him. 'Don't pay no heed.'

'And you!' Karina challenged. 'You ain't exactly welcomed me with open arms.'

Hadley's glance spoke volumes. 'Oh well, if you're lookin' for the phoney huggy stuff . . .'

'No!' Karina realised that the old man had somehow cut the rug from under her. 'What I'm lookin' for is respect.'

'Oh, respect . . . hmm.'

'You mean I gotta earn it?'

'Hmm.'

There was a long silence, during which Sandy and Kirstie couldn't hold back any longer. They began the walk across the corral.

Before they reached the old man's truck, Karina had nodded. 'You're right,' she told Hadley, slinging her bag over her shoulder and marching back to the bunkhouse.

Then as she disappeared through the narrow door she added a last defiant remark. 'Hey boss, you can tell that hothead son of yours that this cowgirl ain't goin' nowhere!'

'So that's OK,' Kirstie told Lady Roseanne later that afternoon. She'd come into the stall on the hour, every hour to check that the patient was clean and comfortable. 'Matt had to back down and apologise to Karina and we all had to admit that we really don't know what happened to you last night.'

About to close the door and slide the bolt shut, Kirstie paused. She inspected the heavy metal fastener and found long strands of white hair caught up in the mechanism, then a streak of dried blood on the rough wooden board beneath. It looked like Roseanne had staggered against the door during whatever struggle had gone on and caught either her mane or tail in the bolt. Also, from the way the wood was dented and splintered, it seemed likely that she'd struck out with her hooves to try and free herself.

Such clues made it look even more likely that Karina's theory about the cuts being self-inflicted was true. 'But why?' Kirstie said out loud, as if the poor horse was able to answer.

She was interrupted by Ben opening the main door and throwing some broken tack into the repair box.

'Hey, Kirstie!' he called. 'How's the patient?'

'She's doing just fine.' Then Kirstie remembered the second reason for her visit to the barn, which was to feed the kitten. 'Ben, did you see Cornbread today?'

'Nope.'

'He's not in the tack-room?'

'No. It sure makes a change not to be used as a climbing frame while I'm workin' in there!' he laughed.

'So I wonder where he is?' For the first time since morning, she began to find the kitten's absence strange. Usually, Cornbread would be at the side of his empty metal dish, miaowing loudly for his food. But today the dish, which was stationed just inside the barn door, was deserted.

No kitten opening his pink mouth wide and reminding her loudly that his stomach was empty. No creamy-yellow ball of fun tripping her up as she came into the barn. No little claws clinging on to the hem of her jeans or wrestling with her boot laces.

'Here, kitty, kitty!' Kirstie strode over to the dish, picked it up and rattled it with a nearby stick. 'Cornbread, quit playing hide and seek. Look, I'm about to give you some delicious dinner!'

Not that there was anything very tasty-looking about the spoonfuls of processed meat she scooped out of the tin. But Cornbread usually raced to gobble it up.

'Here, Cornbread!' she called, tapping the dish with the spoon.

The noise startled a jay in the rafters, and it flapped away alongside the roof-high stack of hay bales. Roseanne too grew unsettled by the rising tone of Kirstie's anxious voice.

Kirstie listened hard. She thought she'd caught a tiny sound that could be a small cat's miaow emerging from some place high in the stack of hay. There again, maybe she'd imagined it.

'Here, kitty!' she cried again.

This time she was more definite – there was an answer floating down from the gloomy rafters. A small, high cat's voice crying out for help.

With a sudden catch in her throat, Kirstie dropped the dish and spoon and ran the length of the barn. 'Cornbread, where are you?'

Miaow! The little cat's pitiful call drifted down.

The rascal had obviously got himself stuck up there, which was why no one had seen him around all day. 'OK, I'm coming up!' she yelled, vaulting on to the lowest level of bales, then scaling quickly up the stack. Soon she was at the top and scrambling along, ducking under the heavy horizontal beams and brushing cobwebs from her face.

'Jeez, Cornbread, what kind of mess did you get yourself into this time?' Kirstie complained, drawn to an out of the way corner by the kitten's cry. Maybe he'd been chasing mice and fallen down a narrow gap between two bales, got himself stuck and had been waiting for someone to climb up and rescue him.

With wisps of sweet-smelling hay tickling her nose, and inching further towards the dark spot, she silently cussed over Cornbread's scatty antics.

'OK, OK, I'm coming!' she grumbled. It was no fun getting dust up your nose and scratching your arms on the rusty nails sticking out of the old wooden beams. By this time, her eyes had grown used to the dark and she could see almost as well as if it was daylight. She spotted where the hay bales came to an end in a musty corner thick with spiders' webs. Chinks of light shone in through cracks in the tin roof, making the dust motes dance and highlighting the corpses of flies trapped in giant webs.

'Yuck!' Kirstie crawled on. She knew she could be only feet away from Cornbread's self-made prison.

His cry grew louder and more desperate.

Then she saw him – bright eyes glinting, hidden as she'd guessed between two bales, but with space enough to crawl out if he tried. It seemed he wasn't trapped after all.

'Hey, what's the problem?' she muttered, delving into the hay to scoop him out.

Cornbread cried as she picked him up. His small body hung limp in her hand, one paw tucked in towards his furry chest.

'What happened to you?' Kirstie gasped, cradling him carefully in both hands. Besides the injury to his front paw, there was a jagged tear in one ear and dried blood caked over his sad little face. And he was shaking from head to foot, cowering in her gentle grasp.

'OK, never mind, let's get you out of here.' Kirstie's soft murmur helped Cornbread get over his fright. She hugged him close and made her way back along the top of the haystack, then down gradually to ground level.

'Ben, fetch Matt!' she called, spying the tall, lean figure of the head wrangler. 'We need more first aid. Tell him it's Cornbread that got injured this time!'

Soon Matt came running with his vet's bag. 'I'm not so hot on small animal work,' he warned Kirstie when he saw the problem. He took Cornbread from her and lay the kitten down on a clean white towel which he'd spread out on a bale. 'But even I can diagnose broken bones in the foot when I see them.'

'What about his poor torn ear?' Kirstie demanded.

Matt cleaned it with a wet sterile wipe. 'There's a chunk missing from the tip,' he confirmed. 'But he ain't gonna fuss about that long-term. Yep, I reckon this patient will live!'

'Thank goodness!' Kirstie sighed.

'You mean you'd actually have missed the pesky little crittur?' Matt teased, doing his best to strap up the broken foot inside an elasticated bandage while Cornbread squirmed and wriggled.

Kirstie gave him a dirty look. 'So what d'you think happened here?'

Matt shrugged. 'A fall maybe?'

'But that doesn't account for the rip in his ear.'

'So he caught it on a nail when he fell.' To Matt this sounded a perfectly reasonable explanation. He finished with the strapping and handed the kitten back to Kirstie. 'That's two patients for you to nurse back to health,' he reminded her, casting a look in the direction of Roseanne's stall.

'Yeah, and two mystery causes,' she added. To Kirstie, Matt's fall scenario didn't stack up. Or at least, she had a gut feeling that it wasn't the answer. 'You don't reckon the two things could be linked?' she asked quietly, stroking Cornbread until his bright eyes began to blink and close. His warm, light body nestled close against her chest.

'Don't see how a horse covered in cuts and a kitten with a broken paw are connected.' Matt's abrupt reply meant end of conversation. Telling Kirstie to bring Cornbread into the house, he strode ahead.

But somehow she couldn't shake off the suspicion that Cornbread's so-called accident did link up with whatever had happened to Lady Roseanne. After all, it seemed probable that the two things had happened at roughly the same time, to judge by the fact that Cornbread hadn't been seen all day.

Slowly Kirstie carried the kitten towards the house. She stopped at the barn door, still deep in thought.

An early dusk was descending over the mountains and forest, bringing stillness and silence, together with a sharp snap of frost. It looked like yet another cold night ahead.

A hard time for the animals and birds of the forest – sub-zero temperatures, the threat of snow. Overhead, an owl swept across Red Fox Meadow,

out on his evening hunt. And in the hills, from
under the thick canopy of pine trees, a lone
coyote howled.

6

Coyotes were on the prowl, no doubt about it.
On Monday evening Ben found fresh prints in
the area of cleared willows by Red Fox Meadow.
Soon after, the night air was full of their cries.

The wild dogs were out there, closing in on the
horses under cover of darkness, circling the
meadow, throwing back their shaggy, wolf-like
heads and calling to the rest of their pack lurking
in the hills.

From the safety of her warm bed, Kirstie
listened. She imagined a huge number of the

scary creatures hunting in one vast pack, together able to bring down prey as big as a deer or foal . . . their pointed faces, coal-black, glittering eyes and white fangs thrust themselves into her dreams and she woke up sweating with fear.

'If it was coyotes who spooked Lady Roseanne and took a chunk out of Cornbread's ear, we gotta do something to keep 'em out,' Karina had told Matt and Ben.

They'd got through Sunday and Monday night without any further incidents, but the mood around the ranch was still edgy. So, come Tuesday, her day off, Karina took it on herself to load up the truck with fence posts and razor wire and while Kirstie was in school, she erected double fencing along the creekside stretch of the meadow.

'Did you get any help?' Kirstie asked her when she got back from San Luis.

Karina grinned. 'Let's just say I didn't notice any long line of volunteers back there!' Obviously proud of her work, she strolled along the bank of the creek, pointing out the places where coyotes would be most likely to crawl through.

'Good job!' Kirstie murmured, beginning to

think that she might sleep easier that night.

'That's not all!' Karina turned and led her towards the barn. 'My theory is that coyotes pick out the weakest or most vulnerable prey. A bunch of horses together in a meadow ain't that easy. Not when you have personalities like Rodeo Rocky and Navaho Joe defending the ramuda. So what does a smart pack of wild dogs do in this situation?'

'They look for a horse that's sick or isolated,' Kirstie guessed, running as usual to keep up. 'You're thinking Lady Roseanne is an easy target, tucked away in the barn?'

'Uh-huh.' Karina explained how she'd expressed this very worry to Matt. 'To me it seems pretty plain that Roseanne should be out in the ramuda, amongst the other guys. Joe would take care of her if any mean crittur crept up unawares.'

Kirstie nodded. 'But Matt didn't see it that way?'

'Nope. His idea is that the Appie's injuries make it doubly necessary to keep her safe indoors. You know how hung up he is about her.'

'Don't tell me! So Roseanne stays in the barn and you've done some extra work to protect her?'

'You got it. Look at this.' Proudly Karina took Kirstie into the barn and showed her a row of new electric lights which she'd strung up along the central aisle. 'I fitted them with low wattage bulbs – night lights – to keep out any sneaky coyote who reckoned he could creep in unnoticed. Plus an automatic light on the outside wall which is triggered by movement.'

'Cool.' Kirstie knew that nocturnal animals such as coyotes would run a mile from the floodlit scene. She paused at Roseanne's stall to look in on her. 'You see this? This is all for you!'

The Appie glanced up from her manger as if to say: *Don't hassle me while I'm eating*. Then she munched on.

'There's gratitude!' Karina laughed, perching on a nearby bale and leaning her elbows on her knees.

Kirstie continued to study the mare. 'Most of those cuts have healed up nice and clean. There's only the one deep puncture wound that we still need to work on.'

'No sign of infection?' Karina took out a strip of gum and began to chew.

'No – touch wood. Matt got that part right at least!'

Finishing her supper, Roseanne turned stiffly on the injured wither and came for some petting. Kirstie obliged.

'How's Cornbread getting along?' Karina asked, still sitting and admiring her handiwork.

'Good. He hops along on three paws, but it doesn't seem to bother him. And he looks kinda cute with a chewed ear.'

'Battle-scarred!' Karina laughed. She jumped to attention as she heard the barn door open.

'Time to drive the feed trailer out to the meadow!' Ben called. 'Unless you want those horses to starve!'

'I'm right with you!' Instead of arguing that this was her day off, Karina jammed her hat down firmly and ran to complete her next chore.

'That gal's gonna bust a gut if she don't take it easy.' Hadley's comment over supper made Kirstie smile.

She'd been describing to the old man and Matt the mountain of work that the new wrangler had got through on her rest day. 'Karina's a one-woman tornado,' she agreed. 'But I thought you'd be impressed.'

'Hadley wouldn't admit it even if he was,' Sandy chipped in. She was on her way out to drive into town to spend an evening with friends. 'When did you ever hear a word of praise pass his lips?'

'Except if it has to do with a horse!' Kirstie added.

The phone rang as Sandy said her goodbyes, so Kirstie got up to take the call.

'For you, Matt!' she yelled from the hallway.

'Who is it?' he grunted lazily.

'Lauren. She's calling from Paris, France!'

The noisy scrape of a chair told her that Matt had sprung into action. 'He's on his way,' she told Lauren, who, far from sounding thousands of miles away, spoke as if she was in the next room.

Within seconds, Matt had grabbed the phone.

'Tell her about Lady Roseanne!' Kirstie reminded him.

But he turned his back and started in with the gooey stuff.

So Kirstie beat a hasty retreat to the kitchen, where Hadley polished off the last of an apple pie, took his hat and left.

Five minutes later, as Kirstie stacked plates in the dishwasher, Matt came back in. Instead of riding on the crest of a wave at the latest communication from Lauren, his face was creased by a deep frown.

'Problem?' Kirstie asked.

He nodded. 'Lauren's grandmother took sick – coronary trouble. She's in the hospital in Denver. They say it's bad enough for Lauren to fly home and visit.'

'Jeez!' The surprise news sounded serious. 'When does she plan to get here?'

Matt absent-mindedly swallowed a last mouthful of coffee. 'Thursday. She already fixed up her flight.'

Under other circumstances, Matt would be thrilled to have Lauren return early. But this was a major family crisis, Kirstie knew. 'You'll be there for her,' she told him gently. 'That's gonna help her through.'

He nodded unhappily. 'Yeah, but there's the Appie to worry about.'

Kirstie jerked the door of the dishwasher shut. 'You didn't tell her?' she said more sharply.

He shook his head. 'And I didn't ring her folks about it. It's too late to do that now. So Lauren's gonna fly in to this big problem about her grandma, plus the stupid injury to her horse!'

For Kirstie, going to school next day was tough. She wanted to stay home and help out, just be there to take care of Roseanne and see Matt through the coming crunch.

But her mom was strict about such things. 'We carry on as normal,' she insisted, pressing Kirstie's schoolbag into her arms and directing her towards the car for the run into town. 'Today's Wednesday, so nothing's gonna happen. And Matt will just have to—'

'I know, he'll have to cowboy up!' Kirstie cut in. Deep down she agreed. But nothing made it easier for her to concentrate on schoolwork and sit through the day when her mind kept straying to Lady Roseanne and the way the puncture wound was healing – to the flushing out with Betadine and Matt's daily shot of antibiotic.

So she rushed back with Hadley, who had picked her up after an errand at the sale barn, quizzing him during the entire journey about Roseanne's progress and asking his opinion about how Matt should break the news to Lauren.

'These things happen,' he shrugged, flicking

on his headlights for the last stretch of the Shelf-Road. 'Horses are always fallin' sick or hurtin' themselves. Ain't a whole lot we can do about it.'

Kirstie fell silent and stared ahead. *Yeah, but what if it was Moondance we were talking about here?* she thought to herself. *Would you be taking things so calmly then?*

The answer was 'No way!', Hadley and Moondance were practically joined at the hip. That was one of the reasons Kirstie was so fond of the grouchy old guy.

'Drive faster,' she pleaded as daylight faded. Her plan to walk Roseanne out into the arena for a spell of exercise would only happen if they beat the frost and the dark.

'I'm goin' fast as I can,' Hadley muttered stubbornly. 'Hold your horses, Missie, if you wanna get home in one piece.'

As it happened, when they arrived it was too late to lead Lady Roseanne out of her stall. The day was gone and Matt decreed that, even with a rug, it was too cold to expose the patient to the cold air.

Accepting the order ungraciously, Kirstie

rushed to get changed then scoot out into the barn. OK, if she couldn't exercise the Appie in the arena, she would spend time working with her indoors!

Crossing the corral in the dusk, she found that Karina's new security light worked just fine. As she passed under it, the beam was activated and shed a pool of bright light in a ten yard radius. Inside the barn, the gentler glow from the string of night lights welcomed her.

Yet the new arrangement didn't seem to have helped settle Lady Roseanne, cooped up in the stall. In fact, she was sounding restless, kicking up straw and barging against the wooden sides.

'It's only me!' Kirstie called, picking up speed to reach her. In passing, she righted the big grain barrel that had been tipped on to its side and left with its lid half-off. She found Roseanne in one of her spooked moods – eyes rolling, ears laid back and tail pressed tight into her rump. Out in the meadow, Kirstie could hear Navaho Joe's distinctive whinny.

'So you don't like being in here all alone.' She spoke softly to the nervous horse and thought hard about what she could do to help. Her first

91

priority was obviously to calm her down and stop her from trampling clumsily around the stall. 'Much more of this and you'll open up those sutures,' she warned.

Still Roseanne clattered and banged around inside the small space.

'You want me to bring in Joe to keep you company?' Since her own presence didn't seem to be providing any benefit, Kirstie's new idea felt like a good one. So she grabbed a headcollar and lead-rope and ran out to the meadow.

Ahead of the game as usual, Navaho Joe was standing at the gate waiting. Impatiently he let Kirstie fasten on the headcollar, then almost pulled her off her feet as he trotted for the barn. Caught by surprise in the glare of the security light, he stopped dead and half reared, once more tugging her arms from their sockets.

'OK, OK!' Breathless, she guided the tough Appaloosa on into the barn. 'You can spend the night here with Roseanne, take care of her, see she doesn't drive herself crazy!'

Even now, Kirstie could hear that Joe's presence in the barn had quietened Roseanne. The noises from her stall were less frantic; she seemed to be listening and waiting for him to show his face.

But, as she chose the stall next door for Joe, led him in and began to fetch fresh straw for bedding, it was the free-spirited gelding who grew suddenly uneasy.

'What is this?' Kirstie said out loud. 'Is this infectious suddenly?'

Joe's ears were straining after sounds undetectable to humans. Every inch of him was alert and tense, his nostrils flared, eyes searching the dark interior of the barn.

'OK, so you want me to take a look around!' If Kirstie read the situation right, she knew that neither of the horses would settle without her carrying out a full investigation of their surroundings. She would climb up the hay bales and take a look, just to satisfy them.

Calmly at first, she bolted Joe's door and began to scale the stack. This reminded her of the evening when she'd found Cornbread hiding between the rafters – a miserable scrap of a thing with a bloody face and broken paw. The memory set her teeth on edge.

Maybe something had made a den up here, out

of the cold. A squirrel, perhaps, or a raccoon. Both of those had claws sharp enough to inflict serious damage on a cheeky kitten.

Or something bigger.

If the attack on Cornbread was connected with Lady Roseanne's injuries then the creature planning to hibernate here in the barn must be large enough to spook a horse.

Kirstie paused to take a deep breath. It sure was dark up here. Hey, and what was it that had just overturned the grain barrel? It could hardly have been Karina or any of the guys, because they would certainly have stopped to stand the thing upright again. Could that have been an animal? Had it figured out that the barrel contained a feast of grain for its supper?

And now that she'd stopped halfway up the hay stack, couldn't she make out small sounds – a tiny rustle, an animal breathing and creeping through the hay?

What if the coyotes had grown bold enough to prowl into the very heart of the ranch? The hair at the back of Kirstie's neck prickled as she crouched in fear of coming face to face with those cruel yellow eyes.

Below, Navaho Joe and Lady Roseanne seemed to have turned stiff and silent with fear.

There it was again – a definite movement in the dark centre of the haystack, followed by a low growl.

Joe went crazy. He lashed out with his back hooves, barged at the bolted door, demanding to be set free.

Lady Roseanne writhed and kicked inside her stall, battering her body against the walls, tossing her head and squealing with pain. The more she squealed, the worse Joe grew, straining at the bolt until the surrounding wood cracked and split. He barged once more and the door gave way.

Then he was in the aisle, rearing up in front of Lady Roseanne, pawing the air with his front hooves. A prisoner inside her stall, Roseanne screamed in agony.

The growling creature hidden in the hay began to erupt out of the stacks. Kirstie saw bales move, thrown to one side as if they weighed nothing. The sight was enough to make her slide and scramble down to ground level, heart thudding inside her chest.

'Matt!' she yelled, above the scream of the

terrified horses. 'Ben – anybody!'

Outside she heard feet running and on top of that horses' hooves pounding along the side of the creek towards the barn. There was a yell – Karina's voice, telling Hadley to open the gate to the corral.

More footsteps outside, more movement from the top of the haystack. And the two horses going crazy.

'Quick!' Karina called, her voice strained as she reined her horse into the corral. 'Fetch Sandy. Tell her we got ourselves a problem.'

Through the open barn door, beyond the flailing hooves and rearing body of Navaho Joe, Kirstie saw Karina pull up Rodeo Rocky in a pool of light. Her face was pale as she flung herself from the saddle and displayed what she'd brought in for them all to see.

'I found it up on Bear Hunt Overlook while I was out clearing trails,' she gasped.

Kirstie saw a large black-and-white animal slung across the front of Karina's saddle, its head hanging, its whole form lifeless.

'One of our spring calves.' Karina explained. 'Somethin' just mauled it to death!'

7

The news on Lady Roseanne's wound was bad. Cleaning up the oozing blood, Matt examined the layers of ripped muscle with a grim face.

'What do we do now?' Kirstie asked him. She was shaken by the new crisis and all the unanswered questions. But for the moment she shelved them and focussed on one priority – the fate of the Appaloosa mare.

Her brother reached into his bag for a shot of painkiller. 'This will ease things,' he predicted.

'Come morning, I reckon we should call Glen in to take a look.'

'Will she need surgery?' This was Kirstie's big fear. Surgical intervention would mean a spell in the veterinary hospital and a list of expenses too long to even contemplate. Yet the wound now looked so deep and wide that they might be left with no other solution.

'That's what I need Glen to decide,' Matt answered, disposing carefully of the used syringe. 'He has more experience than I do. I guess it depends on the site of the wound and whether or not we can find a way to discourage Roseanne from using the muscle until it heals. That's why thrashin' around the stall like this is a major setback as far as her recovery is concerned.'

His muttered words threw Kirstie back into the confusion of events which had followed Karina's arrival on the scene.

With Navaho Joe practically exploding out of the barn into the pool of bright light by the door, Ben had run from the tack-room to take charge of the dead calf.

'It sure is one of ours,' he'd confirmed,

dragging the corpse from Rocky's saddle. 'Here's the HMR brand.'

'Grab Joe, someone!' Kirstie had yelled as the crazy Appaloosa had burst into the yard.

By this time, Matt had been on hand to lay hold of Joe's headcollar and tug his rearing form down to ground level. He'd dug in his heels and pulled with all his weight, while Joe whirled and twisted, dragging Matt halfway across the corral before he'd finally admitted defeat.

Inside the barn, Kirstie had given one quick, panic-filled glance up into the haystack. Expecting to see a large creature emerge from the alfalfa, instead there was zilch – zero! The erupting volcano had gone quiet. It was as if there was nothing bigger than a mouse lurking there after all.

So she'd gone into the stall to quieten Roseanne, dodging her flailing hooves, dismayed at the sight of fresh blood oozing from the puncture wound on her withers.

Meanwhile, the activity outside the door had also quietened.

'Tell me again where you found the crittur,' Ben had asked Karina.

'Bear Hunt Overlook. Within sight of Monument Rock. It's pretty wild territory out there, so at first I thought the calf had maybe slipped and broke its back. But as soon as I rode up close and saw the neck wounds, that's when I drew a different conclusion.'

Ben had turned to include Hadley in the discussion. The old man had limped out of his cabin and arrived late on the scene. 'What does it look like to you?'

Hadley hadn't rushed his reply. First he had studied the wound for a while. 'Could be mountain lion.'

'What about coyotes?' Ben had checked.

'Maybe. If they're huntin' in packs.'

'Bear?'

'Maybe.' Hadley had sounded doubtful. 'We didn't pick up any sightings of bears lately, did we?'

'Whatever it is, this is serious!' Karina had interrupted the post-mortem. 'We got a dozen other spring calves out there. I for one am gonna be upset if this happens again!'

'Yeah, but let's think positive.' Growing practical, Ben had made moves to deal with the calf's corpse. 'Maybe this youngster was already injured before he was attacked. He'd been separated from his mother, say. Or he was sick and weak before it happened.'

'You're sayin' it's a one-off?' Karina quizzed.

'Let's hope.'

By this time, Matt had handed Joe over to Hadley and asked the old wrangler to take the gelding out to the meadow. He'd been on his way to join Kirstie in Roseanne's stall. 'Save the investigation for later,' he'd yelled. 'Karina, unsaddle Rocky and put him out for the night!'

This had broken up the group standing in the pool of light and brought help at last to the injured mare.

And now Matt was saying that Roseanne might have to be hospitalised.

Kirstie drew a deep breath. 'I wish Mom was here.'

'She'll be back soon,' Matt predicted. 'She'll have to make the judgement over what to do about the calves left out in the forest. Maybe she'll decide to bring 'em back in and send 'em to the feed lot a month early. But that's expensive, so she'd have to be pretty sure there was good reason.'

'What d'you think is out there?'

'Probably coyotes, though I wouldn't put money on it.' Matt went through the routine checks of Roseanne's temperature and heart rate, returning to study the puncture wound time after time. He was obviously in two minds as to whether to try re-suturing the gashed flesh there and then.

'Would coyotes come right into the barn?' Kirstie asked, explaining to Matt her suspicions about a creature hiding high in the haystack.

'No way!' he said sharply. 'You wouldn't catch a coyote trapping himself inside an enclosed space.'

'So it must have been something else?' The idea made her shiver. The barn felt dark and dangerous all over again.

'Look, give it a rest, will you?' Medical decisions were the only ones Matt cared about right then. 'I'm gonna give Glen a call, OK?'

Kirstie watched him stride away down the aisle. Something in her wanted to follow – not to be left alone in the barn. But she couldn't desert Roseanne.

'It's OK,' she whispered, resting her hand on the mare's neck. 'I don't plan on going anywhere!'

Lady Roseanne's eyes still wore a haunted look,

and she refused to settle in her stall. With the recent painkiller taking the edge off the hurt, she pranced inside the confined space, ears pricked and listening for the least sound.

So Kirstie was relieved when Karina showed up a few minutes later and began a systematic check of the barn from front to back and from top to bottom.

'From what you say, something sure spooked Joe and Roseanne,' she agreed, shifting boxes and barrels, peering up grain shutes and eventually climbing high into the haystack. 'And it spooked you nearly as bad!' she grinned, taking notice of Kirstie's white, strained face.

'It must've been real big!' She recalled the eruption of bales as the creature moved.

'You sure you didn't disturb the stack by climbing on it?' So far, Karina's search had revealed nothing. 'Some of these bales tip real easy.'

As the wrangler gave a demonstration by upending a bale and sending it slithering down to the next level, doubt entered Kirstie's mind. Maybe she'd imagined the whole thing? After all, she couldn't put her hand across her heart and swear that she'd actually seen a single concrete thing . . .

And yet, Joe and Roseanne wouldn't spook that bad over nothing.

'Karina?' Ben called from the door. 'The boss just got back. You got time to speak with her?'

Karina jumped down from the stack, brushing hay from her shirt and jeans. 'Sure thing.' She crossed paths with the head wrangler, telling Kirstie not to get too wound up over any so-called intruder into the barn.

Meanwhile, Ben reported the latest from the house. 'Your mom and brother are talking to the vet on the phone,' he told Kirstie. 'It seems the opinion is that Roseanne should be kept quiet overnight and Glen will come take a look first thing tomorrow. He says no way should Matt try to re-suture the wound until he's paid a visit.'

'How's Mom taking the news about the calf?' Kirstie asked.

'She's not happy,' Ben conceded. 'She reckons the best thing is to put out an alert to the other ranchers this side of Eagle's Peak. That way, they can send riders out to check on their herds. I guess maybe Karina and I will sleep under canvas a couple of nights to keep a closer eye on things.'

He glanced at his watch and read almost midnight. 'You tired?' he asked.

She nodded. 'Tell Mom I'll be in soon as Roseanne lets me leave!'

'Don't make it too long, huh?' Ben was about to retrace his steps, when on second thoughts he turned around. 'Let me fix up a rota of guys to take turns stayin' with her through the night. How does that sound?'

'Great!' Kirstie felt a wave of relief wash over her. 'I think she needs someone.'

'Yeah, so you wait here until I send a relief. Between us we'll stand guard and fight off all-comers. Like the US cavalry!'

She grinned in spite of herself. 'Thanks Ben.'

'No problem.' Calm as ever, he went away.

Kirstie heard the creak and click of the barn door closing. She saw the security light flick on and off again, listened to the head wrangler's footsteps fade.

Silence descended. She was glad of the row of night lights swinging slightly in the breeze whistling through the open sides of the barn. The moving bulbs cast strange shadows but they were reassuring anyway.

'It's cold!' she whispered to Roseanne, noticing that she was shivering after the shock of recent events. Then she wondered if she should slip off to the tack-room to find a blanket to keep her warm. Maybe not – the rug might chafe against the seeping wound and make things worse.

So she stayed where she was, trying to take the edge off the Appie's nervousness by soothing her with strokes and whispered comments. 'Easy!' she told her. 'Everything's gonna be OK, you'll see!'

Roseanne's warm breath covered Kirstie's hands and arms as she leaned in close and accepted the reassurance.

'And now I can't figure out if we're all crazy – you, me and Joe!' she murmured. 'Does it turn out that we were scared of our own shadows?'

The wind blew and a coyote howled, far enough away for Kirstie not to spring into action, close enough to suggest that the wild dogs might be moving in on Red Fox Meadow as before.

'You know something?' A sudden thought had struck her. 'I just remembered a way to check whether or not it was all inside our heads!'

Sliding smoothly past Roseanne and out of the stall, Kirstie ran down the aisle to the point where the big grain barrel stood. It was upright, with its lid firmly on, but the point was, this hadn't been the case earlier that evening. Quite the opposite – the barrel had been turned over on its side with the contents spilling out.

The dim light allowed Kirstie to see the specially prepared light brown pellets scattered across the walkway and trampled into the dirt by various pairs of boots. She frowned, wishing she'd thought to study the area earlier.

Back in her stall, Roseanne let out a nervous whinny.

'I'm still here!' Kirstie called. 'I'm looking for paw prints!'

She crouched close to the ground, picked out the scuff marks where the barrel had tipped, examined the dirt all around it.

Animal prints! Huge marks showing an almost human shaped foot with five toes and long claws.

Kirstie gasped. She looked again in disbelief. There it was – the print of a full-sized bear!

And the nightmare began again. The electric charge in the air, a fear that you could almost touch.

Roseanne squealed as the bear took advantage of the silence and rose from its dark hiding place high in the barn.

Kirstie ran to the stall, looked up and saw a giant black shape emerge from the hay.

The bulk of the creature amazed her. The female bear was square and massive – black, with thick legs and a heavy, pointed face. At the sight of Kirstie's return, she rose on to her hindlegs and gave a growl so deep in her throat, so loud and long, that both Kirstie and Lady Roseanne froze.

For the bear, now that she was out of hiding, there was only one way out. She must come down the stack into the aisle and beat off anyone who opposed her. So she roared and fell on to all fours, scrambled quickly down the bales as Kirstie re-entered the stall and cowered alongside Roseanne.

It was a terrifying sight: a creature big enough to maul and kill a man hurtling down a haystack to the ground. The bear descended head first, surprisingly nimble for her bulk. Her mouth opened in another roar, showing pointed teeth.

Kirstie tried to prepare herself. There were

rules about encounters with bears, which she'd been taught ever since she was young. With a black bear, you mustn't run away. You must hold your ground. You must stand tall and stretch your arms wide, convincing the bear to back off.

These creatures were not natural predators; the trick was not to run or to alarm it in any way.

But when you stood face to face and heard the roar, when you had an injured horse going crazy in the stall with you, it was impossible to follow the rules.

The bear reached ground level; her smell was powerful in Kirstie's nostrils. Close to, her enormous weight seemed to shake the ground under her padded feet.

Regardless of the danger, driven by an instinct to flee, Roseanne burst forward out of the stall. The door swung towards the bear, sending her sideways against the bottom of the stack, seeming to enrage her. She reared and stood on her hindlegs, jaws open, swiping the air as the mare escaped.

Kirstie was still trapped inside the stall. She saw the bear swerve back into the door, falling on it with all her weight so that the metal hinges

twisted and the door splintered. Kirstie put her hands over her head to defend herself from flying planks, praying that the bear wouldn't choose to attack her head on.

When she dared to look again, the creature was thundering on after Roseanne, swift as she was nimble, maybe even capable of outrunning the injured mare.

Kirstie emerged from the wrecked stall in time to see the light flash on as Lady Roseanne emerged from the barn. The bulky shape of the she-bear was close behind, but she hesitated at the sight of the flood of light beyond the door.

The pause gave the Appaloosa time to swerve out of sight.

The corral was plunged into darkness again and Kirstie heard rather than saw the bear resume the chase.

She crashed out of the barn into a fresh burst of electric light. Rearing up and roaring, she pranced out of range of the sensor, hot on the heels of Lady Roseanne once more.

Kirstie was left helpless and gasping, trying to force her weak legs into action, hardly registering the appearance of Karina in the doorway.

'Bear!' she warned in a choking voice, as she staggered towards the wrangler.

'I saw her!' Karina ran into the barn. 'C'mon, Kirstie, get it together. We're gonna jump in the truck and try to cut her off before she sinks her claws into Roseanne!'

8

Fear drove Lady Roseanne along the side of Five Mile Creek. Loping unsteadily because of her injury, she fled under a clear, moonlit sky, hooves crashing through a thin layer of ice when she swerved and crossed the stream.

The bear followed hard on her heels, her speed giving the lie to her square, solid build. She covered the ground on all fours, seemingly content to pursue the Appaloosa without moving in for the kill.

'Why doesn't she ease off?' Kirstie asked

Karina. They had set off in the pick-up and kept the two animals in view, bumping over the rough trail and splashing through the creek after Roseanne and the bear. 'What's the point of putting Roseanne through this?'

Karina focussed on steering round a sharp bend on a steep incline. She threw the Dodge round like it was a racing car, forcing Kirstie to hang on tight to the door strap. 'I guess the bear sees this as her territory,' she replied through gritted teeth.

'But it can't be!' Kirstie protested. 'This is the first we knew about her!'

Usually there would be sightings of a bear moving in to occupy a new home area, or else telltale signs.

'We've been slow the spot her, that's all. If we'd been thinking straight we'd have dropped the coyote theory and figured out we had a bear stoppin' by.' Karina's crazy driving meant that they were gradually gaining on the two animals.

Lady Roseanne had climbed high out of the valley and was cutting through a stretch of stripped aspen trees towards Bear Hunt Overlook. Even from a distance they could see that she was tiring and beginning to stumble. But still the bear kept after Roseanne, glancing over her shoulder every so often, as if to check that her own pursuers were still in touch.

But then the ground they had to cover changed. The trail grew too narrow for the truck, and the trees too dense.

'What do we do now?' Kirstie gasped as Karina screeched to a halt.

'We follow on foot,' she decided, rapidly flinging open the door and running to pick up a couple of ropes from the back of the truck. 'Unless you got a better idea,' she added.

Kirstie shook her head, though she knew that, as far as a one to one race went, they had no chance of keeping up. Still, they could maybe think ahead of the game. 'If Roseanne is heading along the Overlook, we can bushwhack up here!'

Pointing to a side track that crossed the mountain at an angle, Kirstie assured Karina that it would take them all the way to Monument Rock if necessary.

'Good thinking.' Slinging the coils of rope round her neck, Karina started to climb. 'Keep lookin',' she advised as they gained height.

'Holler if you see anythin'!'

Luckily the full moon cast a strong silvery light. But the going was slippery due to a thick coating of frost. The icy surface held them up.

Twice, Karina lost her footing and had to stop herself from sliding full tilt down the mountain by grabbing on to a tree branch. Once, Kirstie did take a serious tumble. She fell on her side, winding herself as she crashed against a boulder, then feeling the whole world tip as she slewed round and took the slope head first. Again, it was only the vegetation that stopped her.

'Jeez!' she mumbled after she'd slammed sideways into the thick trunk of a ponderosa pine. She scrambled to her feet, dusting off the pine needles and dirt. Her shoulder and wrist hurt, but she found she could stand and make her way up the slope to join Karina. 'Did we lose Roseanne?'

Karina shook her head. 'I can still see her down below.'

The injured Appie had come to a halt on the Overlook trail about two hundred yards from where they stood. Her white coat with its brown markings stood out in the moonlight, and they

116

could tell from the way her head hung low and her sides heaved that she was both exhausted and almost defeated. But for the moment, the bear seemed to have given up the chase.

'Let's go!' Kirstie gasped. Hardly able to imagine the sheer terror Lady Roseanne must be experiencing, she overcame the pain from her own cuts and bruises to take a rope from Karina and press on.

'Hold it!' The wrangler's warning came when they were within fifty yards of their goal. 'This looks like the spot where I picked up the dead calf!'

Kirstie paused to note the surroundings. They were close to a level section of the trail bordered by thick thorn bushes. Beyond the undergrowth, Kirstie knew there were boarded entrances to old mine workings – ideal sites for bears to make their winter dens.

'Right there!' Karina picked out the exact location. Moonlight filtered through the pine tree branches, which cast moving shadows on the stony ground.

Kirstie shivered. It was as if she could smell stale blood in the air. She pictured scavenging coyotes with the same scent in their nostrils, lurking silently in the spiky bushes.

Roseanne stood along the trail, a picture of misery in the dark forest. Danger was everywhere – behind every tree, round each bend. Her hurting body could take no more. She would hang her head and await her fate.

Kirstie advanced slowly towards her. There was still no sign of the bear, though perhaps she was quietly watching, waiting . . .

'C'mon, girl!' Kirstie whispered. She knew Karina was close behind, but letting her make the vital approach. 'I know it's tough, but you gotta let us get you out of here!'

Roseanne heard, but she sank to her knees. She wanted to be left alone; she wouldn't fight any more.

It was a case of going close enough to sling the rope round her neck, of whispering encouragement and coaxing her back on to her feet.

The night shadows flickered over her pale form. Hidden creatures moved in the undergrowth. Roseanne quivered, then struggled up from her knees.

'Easy!' Kirstie breathed. She prayed that the bear had given up the chase, that the noises in the bush came from nervous mule deer disturbed by their presence.

The Appie was gathering herself, lifting her head a little. She responded to Kirstie's voice by taking a few shaky steps.

Then the bush closest to them came alive. Its tangled branches parted and a coyote leaped out. Snarling, springing through the air, it launched itself at the weakened horse.

Roseanne reared and Kirstie felt the rope slip from her grasp then fall to the ground.

Karina ran at the savage creature, lashing out with the end of her own rope. It snaked across the coyote's back and threw him off course so that he landed wide of his prey.

Then, with a last scrap of energy and willpower, Lady Roseanne took off.

She veered away from the group, charging back along the Overlook, then downhill towards the creek.

'She's heading for home!' Karina muttered, lashing out a second time with her rope.

The coyote felt the lash and cowered back

towards the bushes. Robbed of his victim, he quickly slunk out of sight.

There was no time to find the Dodge and overtake Roseanne. Kirstie knew they would have to do their best on foot. 'Pray that she finds her way!' she gasped.

They could still see the mare, stumbling ahead of them down the mountain, making for the creek in the valley bottom. Then they lost her pale form against the white frost of the open valley and spied her again close up against the creek.

'She's doin' good!' Karina muttered, watching Roseanne turn for home. 'I reckon she's gonna make it!'

She and Kirstie cut across the slope to follow.

'It's not a clear run,' Kirstie warned. Knowing every inch of the territory, she realised that the Appie had joined the creek on the wrong side of the boundary fence. 'There's a cattle gate between her and the ranch, and no way round it!'

The worry now was that Roseanne would be too weary and scared to stop at the metal grid. If she tried to leap it and fell short, her hoof would catch in the gap and she would snap the bones in her leg.

So they ran on, skidding down the hill, desperate to catch up before Roseanne came to the gate.

There it was – a rough wooden arch over a metal grate, high fences to either side.

The mare saw it in time. Her stride faltered, then she drew up short, wheeling away towards a high black rock which bordered the cattle gate. A shallow, wide stretch of Five Mile Creek ran to the other side, glinting in the moonlight.

'Good – good!' Kirstie whispered. Roseanne's exhausted brain had managed to work out the hazard of trying to cross the cattle guard.

'Wait!' This time it was Karina's turn to spot the complication. She pointed to the shallow water and two dark animals splashing between the wet rocks. 'That explains everythin'!'

Kirstie squinted to make out the creatures in the creek. Bear cubs! Born early that year, they were the size and weight of an average housedog.

There was no mistaking them in their tumbling, rolling play. Like two clowns in a circus, they wrestled clumsily, fell, then picked themselves up to start over again.

'It tells us why momma bear was so mad with

everyone!' Karina whispered. 'The babies must have been in the barn with her. We upset them in their nice warm hideaway, probably came between her and her cubs!'

Kirstie nodded. 'But once she'd chased us all off along the Overlook, she came back to find them.'

'She's still not a happy bear!' Karina pointed out that the mother hadn't succeeded in returning to her babies, who carried on playing in the creek without a care in the world.

Kirstie turned to look at Lady Roseanne, teetering on the brink of the cattle guard. The body language was the same mixture of exhaustion and terror as before – taut nerves, rolling eyes, heaving sides. Her mane hung limp with sweat; dark blood oozed from her wound.

Then Kirstie glanced up at the rock that bordered the cattle guard.

'Karina!' She grabbed the wrangler's arm.

There, perched on the pinnacle of the fifteen foot rock, was the bear.

She was directly over Roseanne, who had frozen with fear. Hunch-backed, staring down, her small eyes glittering in the moonlight, the huge

122

creature sized up the danger to her two precious offspring.

'Freeze!' Karina whispered as the mother bear stirred on her perch.

She was calculating her next move, getting ready to pounce.

As the bear shifted her weight forward and judged the distance between herself and the terrified horse, Kirstie knew that one leap on to the Appie's broad back, one slash from those cruel, curved claws would bring a swift end to the horse they'd fought so hard to save.

A car raced along the trail, headlights glaring. It hit a bump and took off, landed with a scrape of metal and careered on.

'Matt!' Kirstie breathed.

The bear had delayed her attack to glance round at the approaching menace. Another danger to her cubs had presented itself, so she raised herself on her hindlegs and roared.

The two cubs stopped frolicking in the water. They ran on all fours towards their momma, but stopped at the bankside, confused by the screech of Matt's brakes as he drew up and leaped out.

And still Roseanne was trapped against the gaping grid, between the mother and her offspring.

Taking in the situation at a glance, Matt leaned into the back of the car and drew out a gun.

Kirstie made out the sinister gleam of the long steel barrel and her heart stopped. 'Hold it!' she cried. 'Matt, don't do anything crazy!'

Ignoring her, he raised the rifle and advanced towards the tall rock where the enraged bear stood. He took careful aim in the bright moonlight, capturing his target in silhouette against a starlit sky.

'No!' Kirstie pleaded. There must be another answer.

He took two more steps to make certain that his aim wouldn't fail. Then he curled his finger round the trigger, ready to squeeze.

No shot followed. Instead, the mother bear moved like lightning, launching herself from standing position, twisting in mid-air to avoid the cattle guard and making a run straight at Matt.

Matt adjusted his aim to meet the attack. He lowered the gun and swung his body round.

But he was too slow. The bear charged, jaws

open, eyes boring into him. Kirstie saw the creature overwhelm her brother with a mighty leap. The gun fell to the ground and Matt disappeared under a crushing weight of muscle, teeth and claws.

Karina was the first to move. As the bear stood over Matt, the wrangler ran to pick up the rifle. She snatched it from the ground, narrowly avoiding a swipe from the bear's massive paw, then backed quickly away to a safe distance.

Matt lay motionless, arms spreadeagled, head to one side.

Karina raised the gun and aimed.

Kirstie dropped her gaze.

A shot rang out.

9

'Kirstie, grab a hold of Lady Roseanne!'

She heard Karina throw down the rifle and call out her name. With the gunshot still echoing in her ears, she forced her eyes open.

Roseanne stood, legs braced, head down on the very brink of the cattle guard. Blood had oozed from the open wound and down her chest. She was done in from the brutal chase.

But what about the bear? And what had happened to poor Matt?

Kirstie's gaze flicked towards movement in the

creek. She saw the two cubs racing upstream, panicked by the sound of the gun. They forged through the shallows, kicking up spray which shimmered in the moonlight.

Then she made out the giant, shadowy shape of the mother bear charging after them, crashing through willows and blundering over rocks.

'You missed!' Kirstie turned on Karina. 'She's getting clean away!'

'I aimed wide,' the wrangler said calmly. 'Go fetch Roseanne,' she repeated, flinging her rope in Kirstie's direction. Then she took off her hat and crouched over Matt's lifeless form.

In a daze, Kirstie did as Karina told her. She stumbled towards the grid, then slid the bolt on the gate alongside. Lady Roseanne offered no resistance as Kirstie approached, rope in hand. Making a noose with trembling fingers, she slipped it round the mare's neck and led her safely through the gate.

To her own surprise, Kirstie began to cry. The wrenching feeling in her gut had risen high in her throat and came out as raw sobs. Tears were streaming down her cold cheeks.

What now? Sure, they'd rescued the horse, but

Matt was lying senseless on the ground. And Kirstie was scared that her brother might never move again.

'Hush!' Karina urged her, leaning her cheek close to Matt's open mouth. 'Listen – he's still breathing!'

Forcing herself to look more closely, Kirstie couldn't see blood or any obvious signs of serious injury. Matt's shirt was ripped at the shoulder and there was a long, shallow scratch down his right forearm. An inch long graze on his forehead disfigured his handsome face.

'He's trying to move!' Kirstie whispered.

Eyes still closed, Matt groaned and lifted his head. Then he crooked his knees and rolled on to one side.

'Ouch!' He came round with a sharp yell, jerking one arm across his ribs to protect himself. His eyes opened and he gazed right into Karina's concerned face.

Karina reacted by rocking back on her heels to reach for her hat. 'So Momma Bear didn't eat you for supper?' she inquired.

He groaned and pulled his knees up towards his chest.

She stood up straight and brushed herself down as Matt struggled to sit. Then she flashed Kirstie a wide grin.

Kirstie dried her eyes on her sleeve. The last sob faded in her throat.

Karina winked. 'Though we gotta confess, Momma did have us worried for a couple of seconds back there!'

'Hardly a scratch!' Kirstie told Hadley early next morning. 'A couple of bruised ribs. I mean, how lucky is that?'

They were standing in the yard, waiting for Glen Woodford's verdict on Lady Roseanne. A pink dawn tinted the light covering of clouds to the east.

'The way I heard it, luck had nothin' to do with it.' The old man made it plain that he was up to speed with events. 'More like quick thinkin' on the gal's part to pick up the gun and fire it just wide of Momma Bear's head.'

Kirstie smiled and nodded. 'Matt only went and knocked himself unconscious by tripping backwards over a stone. 'Course, he swears that the bear had him in a deadly hug that choked the breath out of him. Which was why he slumped to the ground unconscious. Any which way, it sure was down to Karina that he came out of it alive.'

'Hmm.' Hadley's grunt said it all. 'It turns out, Karina's a mean shot.'

'Yeah, on top of all her other talents.'

'Did Matt bite the bullet and thank her?' Hadley was curious to know the answer.

'Not right away. He was fretting over Lady Roseanne for quite a while.' Kirstie recalled the worry they'd all shared as they'd led the Appaloosa back to the ranch. She'd limped and stumbled on shaky legs, her withers stained dark with blood.

'It's not every day a gal who's a crack shot saves your life,' he pointed out. 'I reckon the boy needs to recognise that.'

Kirstie smiled to hear Hadley come out and back Karina so strongly. 'You sure changed your tune. Anyhow, eventually Matt did make a few grunts that sounded like thank you.'

Making their painful way towards the ranch, the small, weary group had been met by a worried Sandy and Ben. Sandy had sent Ben back for the trailer to drive Roseanne in along the last half mile of Five Mile Creek Trail. An overjoyed Kirstie had described to her mom the moment of high drama when Karina had fired the warning shot.

'It whizzed clear of the bear's ear!' she'd told her. 'Scared her big time. Karina says she never saw an animal that big move so fast. She just turned and scooted towards her babies, got them running upstream before Karina had chance to get in a second shot.'

Then Sandy had examined Matt's scratched arm and grazed face. 'Next time you go racing in like a knight on a white charger in defence of your girlfriend's Appie, just take a deep breath and count to ten, OK?'

Matt had nodded sheepishly and rubbed the bump on the back of his head. 'Uh-huh,' he'd agreed as Sandy shepherded him into the front seat of the trailer.

That was when he'd paused, turned and acknowledged his debt.

'Thanks for divin' in there,' he'd muttered to Karina, who was holding open the door for him to climb shakily inside.

'No big deal.' She'd brushed it aside. 'It was

just what anyone would've done.'

'So what's holdin' up the veterinary?' Hadley wondered. The frosty morning air was getting through to him, making him stamp his feet in an effort to keep warm.

'He has to figure out if Roseanne needs to go to the hospital,' Kirstie explained. 'Matt's hoping that the answer's no. Lauren flies in from Europe later today and he wants to give her some good news to balance out the bad.'

Hadley shook his head impatiently. 'The way they fuss over that mare is a crime against the equine species!'

She grinned and glanced towards the barn. 'So what's the story with the bears?' she asked, to change the subject. 'Did I hear right – you already spoke with Smiley?'

Smiley Gilpin was the leader of the Meltwater Forest Rangers team, living up at Red Eagle Lodge, north of Bear Hunt Overlook. Half an hour earlier, before Karina had ridden off in that direction to check out the situation around the old mine workings, she'd mentioned to Kirstie that Hadley had already made the call.

He nodded. 'The story with the bears is that Smiley heard on the grapevine that there was a big burn out during the late summer, eighty miles south west of here. It drove all the wildlife out of the area, including two families of black bears.'

Hadley paused in response to a creak and a click from the closed barn door, but it proved to be a false alarm. 'Smiley reckons that one of those two families strayed to these parts and chose Bear Hunt Overlook as their new home.'

'It sure looks that way,' Kirstie agreed. 'So what happens now?'

The old man shrugged. 'No rancher wants bears setting up home anywhere near their cattle or horses.'

She could well understand why not. Look at what had happened on Half-Moon Ranch since the new family moved in. 'One dead calf and a seriously spooked horse is bad news.'

'Forget the calf,' Hadley advised. 'I put that one down to coyotes.'

'How come?'

'Black bears don't eat meat unless they have

no choice. Berries, nuts, roots – that's more their thing.'

'Yeah, and the grain in our barn!' Kirstie reminded him.

'I reckon it was coyotes that found themselves a sick calf, singled it out and brought it down. And the only reason we had problems with the bear and the Appie last night was because Momma Bear was defendin' her young.'

'So how do we stop her raiding our barn from now on?' Kirstie wanted to know. In her own mind she was now glad that Karina hadn't shot to kill the bear, leaving two orphan cubs to cope with the severe winter ahead. Still, she didn't see a way out of the problem if the bears returned.

The question had Hadley stumped too. 'Back in the old days, we'd go ahead and shoot her, no problem.'

Kirstie frowned. 'Isn't that against the law now?' As far as she knew, Black Bears, like Grizzlies, became a protected species after hunters had pushed them to the edge of extinction.

'Yeah,' Hadley admitted. 'These days it's almost against the law to breathe!'

'. . . But?' She sensed there was more to follow.

'But a rancher can still apply to the sheriff for a special licence to shoot a bear that's raidin' his barn and threatenin' his livestock.'

To Kirstie, that course of action seemed harsh. After all, bears, like any other wild creature, had the right to live and do what came naturally. Besides, those two cubs had been darned cute. 'So?' she demanded, as the barn door opened at last and Sandy, Matt, Ben and Glen Woodford strode out.

'It's a decision your mom will have to make,' Hadley told her, limping on his stiff leg towards them.

'You should see Glen work!' Matt's sigh of admiration followed the San Luis vet's black Jeep up the track and out through the gate. 'Jeez, the skill of the guy!'

'Matt wants to be just like Glen when he grows up!' Ben kidded. 'You should've seen his face when he rolled back his sleeves and re-sutured that wound!'

'So, no trip to the hospital?' Kirstie checked.

'Nope. Just the same routine as before – washing out the wound twice daily, antibiotics, total rest.'

Relieved, Kirstie wanted to slip quickly into the barn to visit Roseanne before she went to school. 'How much damage did she do to herself last night?' she asked.

'Well, racing up the Overlook didn't do her no favours,' Matt had to admit. 'But because the wound is deep into the muscle of the wither, rather than across the knee, say, there's plenty of soft tissue to knit back together, layer by layer. Glen gave her a painkiller booster, said she needed stall rest for two weeks, then that should be it.'

No surgery! Kirstie felt her spirits rise at the news. She was able to run into the barn and make a fuss of the patient with a genuine hope that the worst was over.

'You take it easy now!' she told Roseanne, stroking her face and letting her nuzzle against her palm. 'I gotta go into school, but soon as I get back, I'll grab a brush and pretty you up in time for Lauren arriving back home. We gotta get you looking good for her, huh?'

The mare sighed, enjoying the affection. She nudged Kirstie's shoulder with her nose, demanding more.

'No, I gotta go!' she laughed. The quick visit had convinced her that Roseanne had turned a corner since Glen's visit and was already on the mend. She gave her one final pat, then slipped out of the stall. 'You be good, OK!'

Outside in the yard, Sandy tapped her wristwatch. 'You're late!'

'Yeah, yeah. Didn't I miss the schoolbus already?' Kirstie asked hopefully.

'Scoot!' Sandy laughed. 'Hadley's waiting to drive you into town.'

So Kirstie fled into the house to pack her bag and change her shoes. A quick flick of a brush through her long fair hair meant that she was ready.

'Have a nice day!' her mom called from her office as Kirstie dashed out of the house again.

Everything felt almost back to normal – scrambling at the last minute into Hadley's old car, driving out through the gate.

But then she glanced back at the ramuda in the valley below – at Rocky and Joe racing along the fence to say goodbye, at her own Lucky already standing at the gate watching her go. And she felt a jolt of fear for them run through her.

Not to mention her worry for Lady Roseanne now quietly convalescing in the barn.

They had bears on their territory and a long-term problem to solve. Because bears and horses didn't go together – no way!

10

What was to stop Momma Bear from paying a return visit?

The problem plagued Kirstie all through morning classes. OK, so they knew she was only after the grain in the barrel, but how was Roseanne supposed to realise that? As far as the sick mare was concerned, the marauding bear spelt danger.

So, move the grain barrel out of the barn, Kirstie told herself during her history class. *Crisis over!*

Except that the bear would continue to prowl

around the ranch buildings until she located the source of food. And Roseanne's hearing was acute, her sense of smell highly developed. There was no doubt in Kirstie's mind that the Appie would still spook at the bear's presence and possibly do herself more damage.

Glen had prescribed stall rest – peace and quiet. Lady Roseanne should move around as little as possible from now on.

Then maybe Hadley's cool view of the thing was the right one. In the old days they used to shoot bears, he'd pointed out. No messing.

Kirstie shivered, then shook herself. *Try not to picture the moment*, she thought. But it pushed its way to the forefront of her mind anyhow – the glinting barrel of the gun aimed squarely at Momma Bear's head, the cubs looking on helplessly . . .

'There's gotta be something else we can do!' she muttered aloud. The class filed out for lunch, but she decided to slip away to the library to check some facts.

Bears had a home range of seventy miles. Wow, that was a lot of distance! Kirstie sat at the computer, calling up information from a

141

website devoted to Black Bears.

They were fiercely territorial, meaning they wouldn't allow newcomers anywhere near their range. They made several winter dens in recesses under rocks, or in thick undergrowth, but chose one major home den for the big sleep. By late October they were stock-piling food in readiness. Cubs were born in spring and stayed with their mothers during the whole of their first year. Mother bears were protective of their young, and moved into the attack the moment they perceived a threat. They would fight to the death to defend both home territory and their offspring.

'We know that for sure!' Kirstie muttered, scrolling past a cute picture of a Black Bear and her cubs perched in the forks of a stout ponderosa pine.

Then she picked out one final piece of information and stored it in her head. If you took a bear away from its den and dropped it off anywhere within a seventy mile radius of home, it had an almost supersensory method of finding its way back to the original den. However, if the dropping-off point was beyond the magical seventy mile limit, the bear was disoriented and never managed to make its way home. Instead, it would start over, staking out a new home range.

Thoughtfully Kirstie logged off. It was time to go back to class.

That evening, she took the school bus out of town and got off at the Shelf-Road. Hoping that there would be someone there to meet her, she was disappointed to see an empty track. Five miles to walk meant an hour and a half before she could explain the idea that had been brewing and bubbling all afternoon.

She slung her bag over her shoulder and set off doggedly along the ridged surface. OK – now she had her bear rescue plan clear in her head. All she needed was her mom's consent.

But we gotta act fast, she told herself, walking through the shadow of a sheer cliff which edged the route. Before too long, the season of fruit, nuts and berries would end, and the ground would freeze too hard for bears to dig for roots with which to make their winter stores.

On the next bend she listened, then looked up to see Karina raising the dust as she drove the pick-up towards her.

'Jeez, am I glad you came!' she told the wrangler, after she'd pulled up with a screech of brakes. Karina was turning the vehicle round on a shelf of flat ground overlooking a thirty foot drop. Her back wheels skidded perilously close to the edge.

'Your mom said I should come fetch you. She went out with Hadley a while back.'

'Did Lauren arrive yet?' Kirstie was anxious to hear how Matt's girlfriend had taken the news of Lady Roseanne's injury.

'Nope.' Karina successfully turned the pick-up and began to rattle over the rough track towards home. 'Matt went to Denver to meet her off the plane, then take her to the hospital to visit her grandmother. After that, he plans to bring her back here.' She turned to glance at Kirstie. 'You got somethin' on your mind?' she asked shrewdly.

Kirstie nodded. 'I've been thinking. You know it was Smiley Gilpin who found out about the summer burn out?'

'Sure. That's the reason our unwelcome visitors had to flee their home range and head north. Why?'

Bursting to explain, Kirstie rattled on. 'Well,

144

we're gonna need Smiley and his team to help carry out this idea I've been working on. It's my Bear Rescue Plan, which basically consists of cornering the family, catching 'em and driving 'em out way north-west of here to a wilderness area beyond Eagle's Peak!'

'Wilderness area?' Karina mused.

'Yeah, but it has to be more than seventy miles from Half-Moon Ranch, so the bears don't have any chance of working out the way back. It's what you might call a major re-location scheme!'

'And right in line with the preservation work the Forest Rangers are into.' Karina nodded her approval. As she rounded the last bend on the Shelf-Road and the spread of ranch buildings came into sight, she gave an ironic grunt. 'Only one problem,' she added.

'Which is?'

'You remember I told you that Sandy and Hadley drove out together?'

Kirstie frowned. 'Yeah. So?'

'So Hadley took a rifle along. Your mom already phoned the sheriff and got a licence to shoot the bears.'

* * *

'Smiley? Listen, it's Kirstie Scott. We need your help.' Time was short. Karina had by-passed the ranch house in pursuit of Sandy and Hadley, while Kirstie picked up the two-way radio and sent a message to Red Eagle Lodge.

'Yeah, Smiley here.' The ranger's slow voice drawled out a reply. 'What is it? You lost another of your calves or somethin'?'

'Nope.' She hurried to explain. 'Can you organise a team to ship a family of bears out to a new home range? Please, Smiley – it's urgent!'

'Slow down,' he replied. 'How many bears are we talkin' about. When? Where?'

The details weren't important right now, she argued. But in principle, was the answer yes or no?

Smiley hesitated over the practical stuff. 'It's tricky,' he told her over the crackling line. 'Bears are nocturnal, so we need a team out there at night. Most likely we'd have to bring along a vet to shoot a tranquilliser dart into the mother to keep her quiet. Then there's the trailering them out to the remote National Forest area . . .'

'But you can do it?' Kirstie urged as Karina flung the pick-up off the main track and headed up Bear Hunt Overlook. The wrangler had chosen the most obvious place to start looking for Hadley and Sandy. 'Please, Smiley. I need to tell Mom you said yes!'

'Sure thing!' he said at last, sounding up to the challenge. 'Call it "Operation Moonlight" – I'll get on to my guys right away!'

One baby bear was flopped face down on a log, basking in the late sun. His chin rested on the wood, his round ears flicking to keep off the flies. The other rambled on all fours through long, dry, pale yellow grass at the far side of the clearing.

'Where's Momma?' Karina whispered from a vantage point high up on the Overlook.

She and Kirstie had stopped the pick-up as soon as they'd reached the old mine workings hidden behind the thorn bushes. Then they'd searched on foot for signs of the bears.

'Maybe she's inside the den?' Kirstie suggested. Every patch of dappled light and shade in the clearing looked like possible animal movement, but as yet they hadn't managed to spot the six foot long adult bear.

'That wouldn't make sense!' Even Karina

sounded on edge. 'If the cubs are out and about, the mother needs to be there to take care of them.'

The snoozing youngster blinked then raised his head. Perhaps he'd heard their whispered talk, or picked up their scent on the wind. Except that the wind was blowing in the wrong direction, sweeping up the mountain from low in the valley.

The other cub too grew more aware. He sniffed the air then broke into a sprint to join his brother. Together they raised themselves on to their hind legs and peered around.

Within seconds the mother bear appeared. Kirstie and Karina saw her from their high vantage point, emerging from a stand of aspens, her heavy paws cracking twigs underfoot. She stopped at the edge of the clearing, already tuned in to whatever had sent the cubs on to the alert.

'What is it? What's happening?' Kirstie hissed. The bears weren't looking their way, but back into the stand of trees from which the mother had appeared.

Karina shook her head and made a signal for Kirstie to keep quiet.

They ducked lower, but were still able to see

the full-grown bear start to hustle her cubs out of the clearing, up the rocky slope towards the Overlook. *Hurry along to the den!* she seemed to say. *There's something goin' on back there that I don't like the look of.* She kept on glancing over her shoulder as she made the cubs climb, unwittingly shooing them directly towards Kirstie and Karina.

The two hidden watchers held their breaths. What a great chance to step in and corner the bears before they reached the safety of their den! If only Smiley had had his team of rangers and the vet already in position for Operation Moonlight! Instead, they could only watch as events unfolded.

The three bears had almost reached the ledge where Karina and Kirstie were hiding when the cause of their sudden exit from the clearing became clear.

There was more cracking of twigs in the stand of aspens – a hurried approach of human footsteps, then two figures caught sideways on in the full red glow of the setting sun.

The first carried a rifle, which he raised to shoulder level, ready to fire.

Kirstie shot up from her hiding place and

yelled. 'Mom, wait! Don't let Hadley shoot!'

'Are you crazy?' Karina tugged her back behind their rock, but too late to stop her from spooking the bears. The adult gained the ledge and rose on to her hindlegs to protect her cubs, at the same time making an ideal target for Hadley to take aim at and pull the trigger.

Pulling herself free from Karina, Kirstie sprang up again. She remembered the rule – you stood firm, looked brave, made the bear back off.

Eye to eye with the mother bear, Kirstie spread her arms wide.

'Hold it!' Sandy's order to Hadley reached them loud and clear.

'Crazy kid!' Karina muttered from behind the rock. 'Which would you rather do – get yourself shot or mauled to death?'

'Neither!' Kirstie breathed. The bear was ten yards away. Her face was immense and hairy, her small eyes glittering with intelligence. It seemed to take only a split second for her to decide what needed to be done.

Dropping on to four feet, she whirled away from Kirstie and shepherded her cubs out of sight of Hadley down below. Another few seconds of trampling through undergrowth, and all three were gone.

Back to their den. Alive. Ready for Operation Moonlight to begin.

'Thanks, Mom!' Kirstie sank back against her rock, heart pounding.

Sandy stood with her hands on her hips, legs wide apart, while Hadley walked away in disgust. 'Don't thank me, young lady!' she yelled back. 'Come down here and start talking. You've got one heck of a lot of explaining to do!'

'Are you real?' Lauren gazed at Matt wide-eyed. 'I mean, are you seriously telling me that you ran between a bear and her cubs to save my horse?'

While Matt stared modestly at the pointed toe of his boot, Karina stood arms folded next to Kirstie and Sandy. 'Yeah, riskin' their own skins seems to run in the family!' she observed drily.

Sandy had finally got the full picture out on Bear Hunt Overlook. She'd understood right away that her soft-hearted daughter hadn't wanted the bear and her cubs to die. But it had taken some time for Kirstie to explain about Operation Moonlight.

In the end, she'd agreed the plan. 'I might even be able to talk Hadley round,' she'd told Karina and Kirstie on the drive back to the ranch. 'The old guy looks like he doesn't have a grain of sentimentality about him, but to tell you the truth, he was real unhappy about the prospect of shooting those bears.'

'It takes Kirstie to come up with an alternative.' Karina had given her full credit for researching the problem and calling in Smiley Gilpin.

Kirstie had grinned and relaxed back into the bumpy ride home. *Now for a hot tub,* she'd thought, *then the grand reunion between Lauren and Lady Roseanne.*

And this was how come they were all gathered now around the Appie's stall.

They'd had the hugs and the tears as Lauren inspected Roseanne's wound. 'Poor baby!' she'd murmured, arms round the mare's neck.

At that point, Hadley left. He'd been hovering in the barn doorway, pretending not to be interested, but really as curious as everyone else. But the 'poor baby' stuff had been too much for him to stomach and he'd limped off. The security light had flashed on to floodlight his ungracious departure, but neither Matt nor Lauren had even noticed.

'You truly, truly risked your life?' Lauren asked Matt again. She turned his face to the light with her tapering fingers and inspected the graze on his forehead. He showed her the scratch on his arm.

Lauren grasped his hand and held it tight.

But Lady Roseanne objected to the switch of attention. So she nosed in between the loving couple and demanded more petting.

Sandy, Karina and Kirstie grinned.

'I know, Baby, it's been tough.' Lauren gave in. She ran her hand down Roseanne's neck and tangled her fingers in her long white mane. 'But everything's gonna be OK, you'll see. I visited Grandma in the hospital and they've got the heart problem under control. And lovely Matt says you're gonna make a complete recovery! Isn't he an absolute honey?'

Kirstie saw that her lovely brother had the grace to blush to the tips of his ears with embarrassment.

'Hey, Karina and Kirstie are the ones to thank,' he muttered.

Talk about a turn around! After all the criticism Matt had heaped on Karina's head when she first arrived, it must have cost him dear to admit this.

But Lauren had hardly heard. She swept her long, black hair back from her face, stepped out of Roseanne's range and moved in close for another hug from Matt.

'Erm!' Sandy coughed as if to indicate to Kirstie and Karina that it was time to go.

Lady Roseanne stamped and sulked. It made no difference – Lauren only had eyes for Matt.

The three of them made a shuffling exit

down the long aisle of the barn.

' "Isn't he an absolute honey?"!' Kirstie giggled as they reached the corral. A Jeep was driving downhill towards the ranch, its headlights illuminating the horses in the ramuda. 'Are we talking about the same Matt Scott?'

Sandy and Karina folded their arms and stared sternly at her.

'Leave poor Matt alone,' Sandy advised. 'He's lovesick, and there's no known cure!'

Kirstie doubled up in silent laughter.

'Cut it out.' Dragging her upright, Karina pointed to the Jeep. 'That must be Smiley and his team. C'mon, we got us a family of bears to re-locate!'

HORSES OF HALF-MOON RANCH 16
Steamboat Charlie

Jenny Oldfield

Steamboat Charlie, a big black gelding, arrives at Half-Moon Ranch with a bad reputation for bucking off his riders. But Kirstie likes the black gelding's playful nature and happily works with him, until a random gunshot during a forest ride shatters the peace. Was the shot an accident or deliberate? Can Kirstie uncover the mystery – and find out the truth about Steamboat's past?